I0450951

Rockin' Spring

SAMANTHA MICHAELS

SAMANTHA MICHAELS BOOKS

Thank you to my husband for being my number one fan. Thanks to my awesome PA Zoe, Carter Cover Designs for the beautiful cover, my family, and my friends for everything. Finally, thanks to all the authors, musicians, and others who've inspired me.
This book is dedicated to the readers that have taken a chance on me!
A special shout-out to Laura for giving me the name for this series!

Chapter One

Lexi

"Maggie, are you ready for walkies?"

Eighty pounds of black fur comes barreling down the hallway. Maggie, my rescued Black Lab, sits in front of me. I'm so glad it's finally Saturday. My job as an IT professional isn't the most exciting in the world. Sure, it pays well, but I would love to be doing something more exciting.

I fastened Maggie's leash, grabbed a bag of toys, and headed down to the local dog park. Luckily for me, the park is within walking distance of my house. It gives me a chance to get some extra steps in so I don't have to give up my favorite food, pizza. I pulled up my favorite playlist on Spotify and started my journey. I wonder if he'll be there today.

A couple of weeks ago, I started seeing someone new hanging around the park. His shoulder-length dark locks and dark, brooding eyes were enough to make my heart race. Add to that his ever-present scruff and sexy muscles and I was having a lot of naughty fantasies. Occasionally, I would see him with another guy, a sexy cowboy-type.

The cowboy clearly worked out, but I'll pick the bad boy rock star any day!

He wouldn't give me a second look. I have boring hair and let's not even talk about my figure. He can't stop me from fantasizing, though. That's all I have after being dumped by my boyfriend, Bryan the Asshat. I still can't believe his reasons. Fucking dickhead. Leave it to me to find the one man who likes small tits.

I took Maggie off her leash and grabbed a tennis ball out of her bag. After making her sit, I threw the ball. I love watching that goofy girl running and playing and can't think of a better way to spend my weekend, especially now that winter was finally over. No more coat, hat, and gloves/ Now I only needed my hoodie instead of a coat, hat, and gloves. I was watching Maggie run after the ball again when I saw him. My heart started racing just like it does every time I see him.

Damn, he looks especially sexy this morning. I watch as he lets his dog, a yellow lab named Dave, off his leash. Dave beelined for Maggie, as they were the only two dogs in the park. I thought I saw him glance over at me, but I'm sure it was an accident or that I'm hallucinating. I threw the ball a couple more times and watched as two crazy dogs tried to grab it.

I turn my attention back to Mr. Sexy and the rest of the world disappears. The next thing I know, I'm on my ass with two furry faces staring down at me. Then his face appears, and he extends a hand to help me up.

"I'm so sorry. Are you okay?" he said as I'm brushing dirt and leaves off my butt.

"Not the first time that's happened. I have plenty of padding back there."

"Actually, I think you have a nice ass."

"Oh, um, thanks, I guess."

"Dave, come." He sits down in front of me. "Apologize to the nice lady." Dave licks my hand..

"You're forgiven."

Maggie and Dave run off to play. My mystery man joins me on the bench.

"Damien St. James, dad to that clumsy ball of fur."

"Alexis Carter, Lexi for short. Nice to meet you."

"A pleasure to meet you, though I wish it hadn't been like that."

I nod toward the dogs, who are both sitting and watching.

"I have a feeling they planned this."

Damien laughed out loud and my insides turn to goo. A few minutes later, Maggie walked over to me and sat down, panting from all her running. I grabbed the bottle of water out of her bag and filled a bowl so Maggie could take a drink. Of course, as soon as he saw the water, Dave lumbered over and grabbed a drink himself.

"I have to run. Hope to see you here again," Damien said he puts Dave's leash on.

"Have a great rest of the day."

Damn, I sound like a moron.

I watch as Damien puts Dave in the car and heads out. Seriously, jackass, that's all you could think of saying to him. Next time I see him, I'll come up with something better.

After a little more playing, Maggie started getting tired, so I cleaned up the water bowl, gathered our stuff, and put Maggie's leash back on, then walked home. I was dreading it, but I had to tackle the oh-so-exciting chore of my weekend housecleaning. I grabbed some lunch when I was done, then got in the shower. My best friend Melissa was dragging me out to the local rock bar in the next town over.

Melissa and I met way back in kindergarten at New Holland Elementary School. I was sitting there by myself when this chatterbox sat with me. I had no choice but to talk to her. We became inseparable. They got me through the hell that was middle school. When I had my growth spurt, completely bypassing the training bra, and endured endless teasing, she stayed by my side.

High school wasn't much better. Melissa played field hockey and lacrosse. Her athletic prowess made her one of the most popular girls in our class, but she never stopped being friends with nerdy bookworm me. Even now, as adults, I can still count on her. When Bryan sent me packing, she was there that night. We enjoyed way too much wine and way too much ice cream. I never would have gotten through that without my girl.

She was still trying to bring me out of my shell, but I've been in there so long, I don't think it's possible. I'd give anything to walk up to a man and start talking. If I were more like them, I would already have been naked with Damien. Not plain old boring me. I won't have the chance to be with him. I knew if I told my friends about him, they would interfere, so I keep him just in my fantasies.

The thought of getting into the shower makes me sigh. I have become an expert at avoiding mirrors. I'm not overweight, but I'm definitely not what you would call petite. I wish I looked more like the cheerleaders, especially the captain, Amy. They'll always land the men and I'll be on the sidelines. I still never forgot what Bryan said to me.

"I would stay with you if you looked like them," he said.

I walked into the bathroom, closing my eyes until I was past the mirror. After my shower, I got dressed in my usual baggy pants and shirt. Hiding my figure made me feel a little better. Since nobody wants to see me naked, I don't have to worry about anyone discovering what was underneath. I heard a knock as I was finishing up. Melissa.

"Absolutely not."

"What?"

"No more hiding those hot curves.".

Amy handed me a bag.

"Get changed and call us when you're done."

She sat down and played with Maggie until I let her know I had finished getting dressed.

"Damn, girl, much better. I would die for curves like yours."

The kiddies are going to be excited. All we need now is some makeup."

Melissa did my makeup then teased my hair a bit. She was pleased with her work.

"Let's go, the boys are waiting."

We walked into the club just as one of my favorite Def Leppard songs started playing. I kept her eyes on her feet, avoiding the disgusted looks on the faces of all the men had the misfortune of seeing me. Our friend Doug owned the club, having taken over when his father retired.

"Lookin' good, girl," Doug said when I approached the bar.

"I guess. Can I get a bottle of Moscato and three glasses?"

"Coming right up."

I took the wine and the glasses over to the table, pouring three glasses. I watched Doug leave the bar and walk onto the stage.

"Everyone put your hands together for Damien St. James."

My jaw dropped when I saw my tall, dark, and handsome crush take the stage, guitar strapped to his broad chest. The house band started playing Whitesnake's Still of the Night. When I heard Damien's voice singing those sexy words, I felt a dampening between my legs. Fuck, this dude is hot. I felt like he was looking right at me the whole time he sang. I'm sure he was actually looking at Melissa. I returned my gaze to my feet.

Chapter Two

Damien

I heard my name and walked out on stage. Looking out at the crowd, I can't believe I see her sitting there. My sexy dog park chick. I'd wanted so many times to approach her, but I couldn't get her to even make eye contact. Dave made sure we met by taking things into his own paws. I've wanted her since the first time I laid eyes on her. She looks especially hot tonight, showing off those delicious curves. Once I finish my set, I walk to the dressing room.

My only friend, Judd Walker, is waiting for me. When I moved out here from LA, I bought the farm next to his. Judd is an actual cowboy, and his farm is his primary source of income. We found we had a lot of things in common, including our love for rock music and for sexy women. Like me, Judd had yet to find that special someone.

"You'll never believe who was front and center in the crowd," I say to Judd.

"Not the sexy dog park chick?"

"Damn right. I doubt she saw much of the show since she insisted on studying her feet. If she would make eye contact with me, I could make her mine. I want that woman naked in my bed. One of her friends has a body like hers. The other one is skinny and flat, like those annoying models I had to put up with during my rockstar days. I prefer those sexy curves any day. As I'm sitting backstage after a quick shower, Doug, the club's owner, comes in.

"Great job tonight. I think the ladies seemed to enjoy you," Doug said. "Is there anything I can bring you?"

"Some information. Do you know Lexi, the woman who was at the front table?" I asked.

I attended high school with her. Are you interested in Lexi?"

"Yes, I am."

"I always admired her from afar. The other students weren't very nice to her, causing her to close herself off. She deserves a chance at happiness. I hope things work out for you both."

"Thanks, man."

After Doug left, Judd and I walked back out to the club area. The table down front was empty, so I walked over to the bar.

"Sorry, man, they left," Doug said.

"I think we're going to split, too."

I head out, disappointed I missed my chance with her tonight. Guess I'll just have to see at her at the dog park. I'm feeling restless when I get in my car, so I take a long drive, wishing that sexy woman was in the passenger seat. After a couple of hours, I head home. I lay in bed, unable to sleep. All I can think about is Lexi.

I awake the following morning after getting a little sleep. After a quick shower and breakfast, I got Dave ready to head to the dog park. Lexi is almost always there on the weekends, so I hope I run into her today. We walk in and I smile to myself when I see that gorgeous woman throwing a ball for Maggie. I let Dave off his leash and he runs over to play with Maggie. I walk over to where Lexi is standing.

"Saw you at the club last night. I came out to talk to you after I showered. Doug told me you left."

Why did you want to talk?

"I've been attracted to you since the first time I saw you here."

"You need to get your eyes checked."

"Why would you say that? You're stunning."

"Tell my ex-boyfriend that."

"Do I need to kick his ass? Why would he let you go?"

"My boobs and my ass are too big."

"What the fuck! He's the one who needs his eyes checked."

Lexi sits down on the bench near her dog-induced accident, so I sit next to her. I want to kiss her more than I've ever wanted anything.

"So what brings you here to little old New Holland? It's nothing like the glitz and glamour of LA, or so I've heard."

"You mean the land of fakes and phonies?"

"It's that bad?"

"Yeah. The picture they paint in the media is nothing like it is."

"It's quiet here. I hope you don't get bored."

"Not possible with you here."

I see her cheeks redden again, which I find a total turn-on and feel my dick stirring. Down boy, I will him. I know how bad junior wants to be inside her. I want it too and I want it bad.

"You've livened things up for me. I love rock music and seeing you perform last night was the highlight of my year so far. Plus, Whitesnake is one of my favorite bands and you did David Coverdale justice."

"I'm humbled. He is one of my top inspirations."

"I have zero music talent, but I'm a top-notch fan."

"Well, I, for one, am grateful for people like you."

She smiled at me and there went my dick again. I'm going to need to wear baggy pants around her. I get a feeling that there's a naughty girl inside her and I want to find her. She belongs nowhere except naked in my bed. I ache to be inside her, fucking those sexy curves until she's screaming my name. Dave's bark interrupts my thoughts, probably for the best before my dick gives me away.

"I think someone wants to play," Lexi says and grabs Maggie's tennis ball.

I watch as both dogs lumber after it. Hearing her laugh as she watches them makes my heart flutter. What the fuck? No woman has ever had this effect on me. I didn't plan on meeting someone, but damn, this woman is under my skin. Now I need her against my skin. Fuck, I want her so damn much.

"You asked me why I came here. I wanted some rest and relaxation."

"This is the town for that. We have some fun events, but overall, it's just a nice, quiet place to live. I was born and raised her and I have no intention of leaving. My favorite part is being able to experience all four seasons."

"I'm looking forward to that, too. I've always had a secret fantasy of being alone with the woman of my dreams on a cold winter night. I picture us wrapped in a blanket or curled up in front of a fireplace."

"I hope you find her."

"I think maybe I have."

Chapter Three

Lexi

"I'm so happy for you. I'm guessing you're talking to me, so I'll help you get her?"

Damien looks puzzled as he asks me, "What are you talking about?"

"Don't you want me to help you get Melissa?"

"Babe, it's you."

At that moment, Maggie and Dave both bark, as if they understood what Damien just said. We both laugh out loud at the two troublemakers. I'm thinking Dave knocked me over on purpose!

"Me?" I say in disbelief.

"Despite what some jackass said to you, you're quite the desirable woman."

Before I could respond, I felt his lips brush mine, sending all kinds of sensations running through my body. It's been a long time since anyone kissed me, but I'm remembering how much I like it. When I feel his tongue tickle my lips, I open for him. I feel his tongue exploring my mouth, setting me on fire between my thighs. The rest of the world disappears when he caresses my face.

"I want you," I hear myself say. Holy shit, did I just say that?

"I've wanted you from the second I laid eyes on you."

Something awakens inside me, thanks to this sexy man. "Take me back to you house." Who am I right now?

"Are you sure?"

"I've never been more sure of anything."

We put Maggie and Dave's leashes on and walk to the parking lot.

"Do you want to follow me?" he asks.

"I live close, so I walked here."

"My car is right there," he says, pointing at a blue Ford Escape.

We load both dogs in the backseat and he drives. The ride over there gave me plenty of time to think, not always a good thing, and by the time we got to his house, I had freaked myself out.

"Are you sure you want me? I'm afraid I'll disappoint you when you see me."

"I've already seen you and you're stunning."

"No, I mean with no clothes on."

"I'll just have to prove to you how much I desire you."

I take a deep breath and exhale, trying to calm myself. He pulls into the long driveway leading to his gorgeous farmhouse. It's always been my dream to live in a house like this. He parks and we get the dogs out of the back. We walk inside and the house looks pretty much how I would picture a bachelor pad to look. The living room is littered with music magazines and other memorabilia. I notice the two-piece couch and start thinking about how much fun we could have there.

"You want a tour?" Damien asks.

"Just of the bedroom," I respond. Who are you and what did you do with Lexi?

He pulls me close and kisses me, this time with a lot more passion. Our tongues intertwine as I feel his hands move down my back and land on my ass. He squeezes and deepens his kiss. Like it did at the dog park, the rest of the world disappears except for us. He breaks the kiss and leads me to his bedroom. My eyes go wide at the king-size bed with red satin sheets. At that moment, I can think of nothing other than feeling them against my skin.

"Come lay with me," he says.

We both remove our sneakers and socks, then lay down together. He pulls me in close once again and I feel those sexy lips on mine. He runs his hands all over my body and I feel like I'm floating. All my nerves from earlier are gone, a miracle. I feel his hands slide under my t-shirt, setting my skin on fire. He lifts my shirt and opens my bra, freeing my way-too-big boobs.

"Fuck, Lexi, you're the sexiest woman I've ever laid eyes on."

My shirt and bra hit the floor, followed by his shirt. Holy shit, that's the sexiest chest and arms I've ever seen. I feel his lips grazing my neck and I feel a warmth return between my thighs. His mouth finds my boobs, and he sucks on them, his tongue flicking my hard nipples. I hear myself emit a soft moan. He opens my jeans and tugs at the waistband. I lift my ass up and my jeans and panties are gone. He just stares at me.

"Baby, I need to be inside you, but first, I want to taste you."

"Oh, Damien," are the only words I can recall at this moment.

He slides down my body and opens my legs, lowering his head. I feel his tongue between my folds and I gasp at the sensation. His tongue feels so good between my legs and I moan. I'm aching to feel him inside me. I'm also dying to see what he's packing in those sexy jeans.

"Mmm, so good," I moan.

He licks me harder and I feel myself coming undone. Sweet lord, I've felt nothing like this before. He slides a couple of fingers inside me and that's all it takes to send me over the edge. I come all over his mouth and hands as I cry out in ecstasy.

"Baby, that was so hot," he says.

"So good."

"Tell me what you want now."

"I want you inside me, please."

I watch him stand, so I slide to the edge of the bed and unfasten his jeans. When I see he is not wearing underwear, I smile. My eyes go wide when I slide his jeans down. Holy shit, he's huge. I've never been with a man who's even come close. I watch as he steps out of jeans. All I can think about is tasting him like he tasted me.

I lean in and wrap my mouth around him. I'm determined I'm going to handle his entire length, so I take him all the way into my mouth until my mouth is against his body. He tastes so fucking good as I run my tongue along his shaft, tasting his delicious pre-cum.

"Damn, babe, nobody's ever been able to handle me like you are."

I stroke his cock with my mouth a few more times.

"You taste amazing, but I wanna feel you inside my pussy."

"Babe! Get on your back and spread those sexy legs."

I lay down then open my legs as far as they will go. My pussy is throbbing for him and reach my arms out to pull him close. His dick enters me and it takes my breath away. Damn, he feels incredible and holy fuck, he fills me. He slides in and out of me as I rake my nails down his back and onto his hot ass.

I want him as deep inside me as possible, so I grab his ass and try to pull him closer. Part of me can't believe I'm in his bed, writhing beneath him as he fucks my brains out. He is the sexiest man I've ever seen. Not to mention him being a rockstar, which is like a dream come true for me. I sure as hell hope I don't wake and find out this is a dream. I feel him pump me hard as his breathing shallows.

"Oh, Damien, feels so good. Fuck me harder, please."

"Fuck, babe, I've never been inside a woman who feels as amazing as you," he growls, as I feel him empty himself inside me.

Chapter Four

Damien

I sigh then lie down next to her and pulling her close. I've had plenty of sex, but nothing has ever felt quite like this.

"Babe, so good," I say. Am I falling for this woman? No, I can't. This needs to stay casual.

"Mmmm, I've never felt like this before," she whispers.

I hear her stomach growl and watch as her cheeks redden. Every damn time those cheeks redden, I get turned on again.

"Would you like to go out and grab some lunch, babe?"

"Oh, I guess my stomach gave me away. I'd love to."

I grab her some tissues to clean up, then we both get dressed. I watch her, unable to get enough of that sexy woman. I want her back in my bed as much as she's willing. I won't let myself fall in love again, but I'll be damned if I will not fuck that woman every chance I get.

"What are you hungry for?" I ask her.

"You."

"Damn, babe!"

"I love pizza."

"Me too, and I worked up one hell of an appetite."

"You can have me for dessert, if you want more."

"Fuck, babe."

We get in my car and head out to one of the local pizza places. I glance over and see her sitting there with a huge smile on her beautiful face. I feel my heart skip a beat that I'm the one who put it there. STOP IT! You cannot fall for this woman. It will only end in heartbreak, just like every other relationship has. But she is the woman of my dreams. Fuck, what's wrong with me?

We go inside and I see her friend sitting at a table towards the book. Two sets of eyes go wide when they see Lexi with me. I look over at her and she's staring down at her feet. I walk us to an empty table as far away from them as possible so I can talk to her.

"Why are you always looking down? Your face is beautiful. You need to show it."

"You think so?"

"Babe, I meant everything I said."

"Thanks."

"I think your friend's headed this way."

"Shit. I love them, but they're nosy."

"Let me do the talking. I wanna have a little fun."

"Uh oh," she says, laughing.

"Well, well, well, what do we have here?" Melissa says.

"Mel," Lexi warns.

"I'm having lunch with your friend," I say, trying to suppress a smile.

"I can see that. I meant, are you friends or something else?"

"We're fuck buddies," I say.

I glance over and Lexi's mouth is hanging open, as is Melissa's.

"Excuse me?" Melissa says.

"I just fucked your friend and now we're here eating lunch."

Lexi has moved on to trying not to laugh. I'm glad she's not mad at me for saying that.

"Well, um, enjoy," Mel says and they walk back to her table.

Lexi can't hold it in any longer and bursts out laughing. I hear her laugh so hard, she snorts, and it's the cutest thing I've ever heard. I need

15

to get her doing that more. A few minutes later, our pizza comes, which we polish off. We're sitting there waiting for the check when Lexi brushes my hand with hers.

"I need to work off some of that pizza."

"Have somethin' in mind?"

"I wanna fuck again. We are fuck buddies, after all." She flashes a wicked smile and my dick stirs.

After we pay the check, I drag her out of the restaurant. I can't get us back to my house fast enough. We're inside my bedroom and clothes are flying everywhere. We lay down on the bed and I pull her against me, kissing her hard. She moans and jams her tongue into my mouth. She is not that shy woman I first saw at the dog park. I'm about to move on top of her when she stops me.

"My turn," she says and pushes me on my back.

I watch as she climbs on top of me, her amazing tits right in my face. She takes her hand and grabs my dick. After a couple of strokes, she puts my dick inside her and starts riding me, sexy tits bouncing like a wild woman. Fuck, watching her on top of me is incredible. It's like watching porn, but I'm the one getting fucked.

"Fuck, babe. I love watching those sexy tits."

I feel her pace increase and I know she's getting close to exploding. I reach up and stroke her clit with my thumb.

"Oh, fuck, Damien," she screams as she explodes around my dick. She collapses down on my chest, hers heaving.

I grab her ass hard and thrust in and out until I fill her again. She lays down next to me and puts her head on my chest. I can feel my heart swelling again. Fuck, I need to fight this, but she's making it difficult. I hear her laugh.

"What's so funny?"

"I started thinking about the look on Melissa's face when you said we were fuck buddies."

"I couldn't help myself."

"It was great. I imagine I'll be hearing from her. I love her, but she's kinda busybodies."

"Not a fan of people who mind everyone else's business."

"Me either. I never liked gossip, especially because I was often the subject."

"Same. I wore my heart on my sleeve and I paid the price. Another reason I had to get as far away from LA as I could."

"You picked the right place for that."

I look over at the beauty lying in my arms and think to myself, I sure did. If only I could give my heart to her.

"It was what I needed."

"Quiet, relaxing, and you found someone to fuck."

"Babe!"

Lexi yawns, so I pull the covers over us. She falls asleep on my chest. I watch her as she sleeps, and there goes those feelings again. How am I going to fight this unless I stop seeing her? But, I don't want that. I enjoy seeing her play with the dogs at the park, and shit, having her in my bed is incredible, but I might not have a choice. I just can't risk another heartbreak. Fuck, that whore ruined my fucking life. I feel her stir awake a little while later.

"I'm sorry," she says.

"For what?"

"Falling asleep."

"Musta been all that bouncing."

"Ha ha. I feel like I need a shower."

"Me too. Let's go."

"Together?"

"Yeah."

"I can't do that."

"Why not?"

"You'll see me naked."

"Babe, we've fucked twice today. I've seen you naked."

"But laying down hides stuff."

"Listen to me, please. Stop it! You're gorgeous and sexy. If someone couldn't see that, they're the one with something wrong. I want nothing more at this moment than to take a hot, steamy shower with you."

Chapter Five

Lexi

I can't believe I'm doing this. I've never showered with anyone. But something about Damien makes me more comfortable with myself and I follow him into the bathroom. He takes my hand and helps me into the tub, then joins me. He pulls me close as the water runs down our bodies. At that moment, I forget why I tried to resist this.

Damien grabs a bottle of shower gel and squirts some in his hand. He runs his hands all over me until I'm covered with lather. I feel a wetness between my legs and not from the water. His big, muscular hands feel so damn good on my skin. He slips his hand between my legs and holy fuck.

I grab the bottle and return the favor. I spend extra time on his sexy ass and muscular back. He groans and I feel his dick growing. I run my hands down his "v" and graze his dick.

"Keep that up and I'm taking you back to bed," he says in that low gravelly voice I love so much.

"You won't hear me complain."

After we're both covered in lather, we stand there holding each other as we let the shower head rinse us off. I find myself powerless when he's touching me. Once we're all rinsed, he turns off the water and steps out. He looks like a god standing there, water dripping down his naked body, and my mouth waters. He helps me back out of the tub and wraps me in a large, fluffy towel. The fabric feels amazing against my skin. But nothing compared to how he feels. We walk back to his bedroom and get dressed.

"You up for a quiet evening?" he asks.

"What'd you have in mind?"

"I'd love to see your house now. Maybe we could get takeout and watch some TV."

"That sounds perfect. How about Chinese?"

"One of my favorites."

"I like to order a bunch of different things, so I have choices and leftovers, like on one of my favorite shows, Gilmore Girls."

"I like the way you think, babe."

We order the food, then load the dogs in the car and drive to the restaurant. Damien grabs the food while I wait with Maggie and Dave. I give him directions to my house and we get back on the road. We pull into my driveway and head inside. Damien fixes Dave's dinner while I get Maggie's food ready. After the dogs eat, we unpack our food and make up our plates.

"What do you feel like watching?" I ask.

"Have you watched Lucifer?"

"All except the last season."

"Same here."

"Lucifer it is."

I grab my remote and bring up Netflix. We end up sitting there and binging the entire last season. I'm gonna miss that one. If the devil looks like Tom Ellis, you can send me straight to hell. I yawn and wonder how the fuck I'm going to get up for work in the morning.

"Shit, I'm going to be a zombie tomorrow."

"Blow off work. Spend the day with me."

"I can't do that."

"Be a rebel, babe. I'll make it worth your while."

"I like the sound of that."

"Good. Get your hot sexy ass in your bedroom."

We race to my bedroom and rip each other's clothes off. After about an hour, we're spent, drenched in sweat and other fluids. After a quick shower together, we head back to my bed. I leave a message on my boss's voicemail, then we fall asleep together, both dogs laying on the floor at the foot of my bed. The next morning, we grabbed breakfast and fed the dogs, then took them for a walk over to the dog park.

"So," he says when we sit down on a bench, "I realized we don't know that much about each other."

"Well, we've been busy doing things."

"Which has been fun, but I would like to know a little more about you."

"Nothing as exciting as you, I'm sure."

"I bet that's not true. I've found you quite exciting."

"In bed, but that's it."

"Babe, you're awesome."

"Okay. Are you sure you want to know?"

"Yeah."

I take a deep breath and start. "I had a pretty tough time of things throughout school. I was that tall, awkward kid that everyone picked on. Melissa wanted to be my friend, but she was always the popular ones. I was just the shy, quiet, nerdy bookworm. It didn't help my case that I've these damn boobs since elementary school.

I never even had a date until college. I graduated from Penn State with a bachelor's degree in IT, then earned my master's. I love being in IT, though I still run into men who don't think women belong there. It's not as exciting as being a rockstar, but I enjoy and it pays well.

I've never been married or even proposed to. I've told you a little about my ex, Bryan. He hurt me when he did what he did to me, but looking back, I think he did me a favor. Let's just say I did not know how good sex was until you. Past that, my life consists of hanging out with Maggie or being dragged out to watch my friends flirt with every man they see while I sit and get ignored.

"Babe, not sure who all these men are, but damn, they do not know what they've been missing."

"I hope you understand a little more about why I was so skeptical of you at first. Nobody has ever picked me before and it left me feeling like I was being setup or pranked."

"I get it. I'm glad you let me prove to you I wanted you."

"I'm glad too! But now, it's your turn. I wanna know what makes you tick."

"In due time, but I have more questions for you first. What about family? You didn't mention them, so I'm curious."

"My parents never got me. They were more like my friends. My dad was the star quarterback, and my mom was a cheerleader. They were both outgoing extroverts and somehow they created me. Other than enjoying watching hockey, sports weren't my thing. I preferred having a book in my hands. We just co-existed and I had no siblings, so not much of a family life. Then when I graduated from high school, their gift to me was to kick me out. I've been on my own since 18. It wasn't always easy, but here I am.

My life has been boring overall, but then something happened. This tall, dark and handsome rockstar sought me out, fucked my brains out, and awakened something inside me I didn't even know existed.

Before I can stop it, my eyes spill over, releasing a lifetime's worth of sadness and never feeling like I belonged anywhere. I look away, but not fast enough, and I feel a pair of powerful arms pull me close.

"I'm sorry," I say, sniffling.

"Nothing to be sorry for."

"Thanks."

We play with the dogs until they get tired, then head back to my house. I'm standing in the kitchen when Damien comes over and wraps me in those sexy tattooed arms I love. He sees the chocolate bar sitting on my counter and a wicked smile appears. He grabs the candy bar and heads to my bedroom.

Chapter Six

Damien

I'm standing in her bedroom waving the candy bar around when she walks in.

"Just what are you planning to do with that?" she asks.

"Get naked and lie down, if you wanna find out."

"Mmmm."

I watch as my sexy woman strips and lays in the middle of her bed. I open the candy bar and break it into little pieces. Starting between her sexy tits, I put pieces of the chocolate down her body, the last one right above her hot pussy. She watches me, licking her pouty lips as I strip for her.

I walk over to the bed and lie next to her. I lean my head down and grab the piece of chocolate between her tits, licking each one as I eat the candy. I grab the next piece then kiss her hard, the chocolate melting on ours tongues. I run my tongue down her body, grabbing each piece with my teeth as I go until I'm at the last piece. I pick the last piece up and feed it to her.

"Yummy."

"Not as yummy as what I'm about to eat."

I watch her spread her legs, giving me a full view of my favorite part of her body. I lower my head between her sexy thighs and run my tongue over her clit. I hear her moan as she writhes beneath me. Fuck, she tastes like heaven. I suck on her like she's a sweet, juicy peach. I feel her body quake as she comes hard, her hips bucking. She sighs as her body goes limp.

"So fuckin' good," she moans.

I move on top of her and kiss her hard as I slide inside her. I fuck her hard and fast. Her tight pussy feels so fuckin' good wrapped around me. I empty inside her then lay next to her. After a quick nap, we shower and grab some of the leftover Chinese food, then sit down and watch some TV. I love and hate how comfortable I feel around her.

She yawns and says, "I guess we better call it a night. I need to get some sleep so I can be productive at work tomorrow."

"I understand."

"Maybe we could hang out tomorrow night?"

"Not sure."

She looks down at her feet. I feel awful, but I need to take a break before I get in any deeper. I get Dave's stuff together, give her a quick hug goodbye, and drive home. I'm feeling restless when I get inside, so I hit my home gym and get a good long workout in. I grab a quick shower, then head to bed. I need to look for work tomorrow, so I want to get a decent night's sleep.

The next morning, after breakfast, I take a ride to neighboring Lancaster to see if anyone has a help wanted sign. He saw a sign in the window of the popular pet store, Rockin' the Fur, so he went in. The other side of the store was a vintage record shop, owned by musician Mikael Alfredsson and his wife, Hannah.

"May I help you?" the employee named Kurt asked.

"I saw you had a help wanted sign, and I'm looking for work."

"Which store do you prefer?"

"I'm willing to work at either, but I have more experience with music. I'm a retired rockstar."

"We get a lot of them around here. Here's an application. Have a seat at the table at the end of the counter and let me know when you're done."

"Thank you."

The whole time I filled out the application, all I could think about was the hurt look on Lexi's face this morning. I feel awful, but it's better than me breaking her heart later. I finish filling out the application, then walk over to Kurt. He asks one of the other employees to cover the counter and takes me back to his office for an interview. After we finish, he offers me the job on the spot and when I accept, he takes me over to the record store area.

"Cherie, I want you to meet Damien. I've just hired him to help you out on this side of the store."

"Thanks, Kurt. Nice to meet you, Damien."

"Nice to meet you."

"Damien will start next Monday and you'll be training him."

"Sounds great. I'm happy for some help. See you next week."

"Looking forward to it."

"I'll walk you out, and we'll see you at 9 next Monday morning."

"Thank you."

I head home, pick up Dave and take him over to the dog park. I want to make sure I'm here and gone before Lexi and Maggie come over. I know Dave enjoys playing with Maggie and I sure as hell love playing with Lexi, but how I feel about her is scary. After spending about an hour playing with Dave, I go back home. Lexi calls and texts several times, but I don't respond. The rest of the week and weekend are more of the same. I almost give in a couple of times, my dick aching to be inside her, but I stay strong. At least when Monday rolls around, I can focus on work.

She left me a message Sunday night that tore my heart out.

"Hi Damien. This will be the last message I'll leave you. I'm sorry for whatever I did to upset you, but I can take a hint. I wish you the best, and I'll miss you."

It took every ounce of self control not to drive to her house and fuck her until she couldn't move. Instead, I did a super-intense workout, then headed to bed, so I was well-rested for work in the morning. My cell phone alarm goes off at 6:30 Monday morning. I feed Dave and take him for a walk. Of course, Judd is already up and working hard on his farm.

"Mornin' Damien," Judd says.

"Hey, man."

"Where's your lovely lady?"

"Not where I wish she was. I fucked up, man."

"Then fix it. That's not the type of woman you let go."

"Thanks, man."

Judd gets back to work, so I finish my walk. I get home, shower, and get dressed. I get to the store at 8:30, so I run to the restaurant across the street, Garden of Eden, to grab coffee and a muffin. I sit in my car and finish breakfast, then head into the store at 8:45.

"Good morning," Kurt says.

"Good morning."

"I have some forms you need to complete, then I'll turn you over to Cherie."

"Sounds good."

After we completed all the paperwork, Kurt walked me out to the music area, where Cherie was just getting things set up for the day.

"All yours, Cherie,: Kurt tells her.

"Thanks. You ready to get started?" she asks.

"Yes ma'am," I say.

"Rule number one, don't call me ma'am," she teases.

"You got it."

"Kurt told me you know your music, so I don't need to go over that. The last person who worked here knew nothing except boy bands. Ugh."

I laugh and reply, "No worries there."

"Most of what you'll be doing is helping customers find items and running the register. Customers will sometimes ask for recommendations. You are free to recommend based on your taste. Kurt's only rule is that you first inquire if there is anything they are uncomfortable with, such as language, sexual content, stuff like that."

"That makes sense."

"Looks like we have a customer now. Come with me."

"Welcome to Rock the Fur. How may I help you?"

"I'm looking for a hair metal band from the 80s, The Wolves."

My ears perked up. I can't believe someone is asking for that band.

"Right this way, sir."

I stifle a smile as I follow behind Cherie and the customer. I can't believe when I see vinyl copies of all six albums released by the band.

"Which album were your looking for?" Cherie asks.

"I'll take them all."

"Wonderful. Pick out which copy of each record you want, then bring them up front."

"Thank you, miss."

"My pleasure."

I follow Cherie back to the counter.

"Once he brings his purchases up, I'll walk you through how the register works."

"Sounds great."

A few minutes later, the customer brings a stack of records up to the register.

"Great choices, sir. I'm training a new team member today. If you're not in a hurry, would you mind me using your sale to walk him through the process?" Cherie asked.

"Please, take your time. I was new at my job once and remember what it was like."

"Thank you. Damien, watch what I do."

I watched as Cherie showed how to complete the sale. She bagged up the albums and handed them, along with the receipt, to their customer.

"Thank you, miss." Turning to me, he said, "Did I hear correctly that your name is Damien?"

"Yes, sir."

He pulls one album out of the bag and asks, "Is this you?"

I smile and respond, "A much younger version, yes."

"Wow. Would you mind signing the records I just bought?"

I look at Cherie. "Is this okay?"

"Yes, of course."

"Then, sir, I'm happy to sign these."

Cherie hands me a marker so I can sign the albums. When I'm done, I hand the bag back.

"Would you mind taking a selfie?"

"Not at all."

After the customer snaps a picture, he smiles, thanks us and leaves.

"Why didn't you tell anyone who you were?" Cherie asks.

"I prefer leaving the past in the past."

"I hear you."

The rest of the day sped by. I enjoyed getting to talk about music with the customers. At the end of my shift, I walked over to the pet shop and came face to face with Lexi.

Chapter Seven

Lexi

W hat the hell is he doing here? Then I see it. He's wearing a name tag. Well, fuck him, I couldn't care less what he does.

"Hi, Lexi."

"Damien," I respond, then turn and walk away. I need to stay focused on why I'm here, so he doesn't see me upset. I walk down the aisle to the dog food and grab the 30 pound bag.

"Let me help you."

"I'm fine."

I walk past him and carry the bag to the counter. After paying for my purchase, I go to grab the bag to carry it to my car when Damien grabs it first.

"Put that down."

"Nope."

I watch in disbelief as he marches out of the store and walks to my car. I have no choice but to follow him. I unlock the door and he puts the bag in the backseat. He stops me when I try to get in the car.

"Let me explain."

"Not interested."

I get in my car, shut the door and pull away, leaving him standing there staring. I fight back tears the entire way home. Seeing him made me realize how much I've missed him. Asshole. He cuts off communication with me and I should just stand there and let him feed me bullshit. Nope, not this girl. I'm about to pull into my driveway when I hear a text message come in. Once I'm parked, I check my phone and see a message from Mel.

"I'll be over at five."

I'm especially grateful to my friend after today. We're having a girls' night, filled with pizza, wine, and a Friends marathon. This will be what I need to take my mind off that dickhead. I get changed, then take Maggie for a walk before the girls arrive. A little before five, I hear a car door. I'm relieved to see Mel with plenty of pizzas and plenty of wine. We get ourselves set up in my living room and put Friends on while we have dinner.

"How come you have me here instead of that sexy man?"

"Total ghost job."

"That sucks, girl."

"It does. I hate to admit it, but I miss him."

"I get that. He's fuckin' hot. I want deets about his bedroom performance."

"Holy shit."

"You gotta give me more."

"Well, for starters, his dick is huge. And damn, he knows how to use it. I felt things I didn't even know existed. And oh my god, what he did to me with his tongue. I hate that I'm never going to feel that again, but I'll figure out a way to get over him. I hope."

"I have to ask. Did you tell him what happened with Bryan?"

"Sorta. He knows about Bryan hating my looks."

"But not the other thing?"

"No. And I don't want to talk about that anymore."

Melissa sits next to me and hugs me. That's all it takes. My face crumbles and my eyes overflow. How did I let my feelings get this far? This was supposed to be casual sex and nothing more, yet here I go, letting myself turn it into more than that. I'm tired of having my heart broken. I shake as the tears come hard and fast.

"Talk to me."

"I can't believe I let myself do this again. I fell in love with that asshat Bryan and look where that got me. This time, I decide to keep things casual, but Damien was so sweet to me I fell in love again. Fuck, there's something wrong with me."

"There is not. You're a romantic-at-heart Pisces and it's what I love most about you. I might be wrong, but when I saw you two in the pizza place, I swore he was looking at you the same way you were looking at him."

"So, why did he stop responding to me?"

"How much do you know about him?"

"We hadn't got that far. The last time we were together, I told him about me, but we never got to him. I was planning to ask him the next time we were together, but of course, that didn't happen. Then today I stopped by Rock the Fur to get a bag of food for Maggie, and who do I run into?"

"You're kidding."

"If only. He had a name tag on, so he was working there or at the record store. He grabbed the bag of dog food after I paid and walked to my car. He tried to explain, but I wouldn't let him talk and I sped off."

"I hate to say this, but maybe you should hear him out."

"You've got to be kidding me? Why the fuck does he deserve that? He ghosted me."

"I know, sweetie, but maybe he had his heart broken, too. Maybe he's as afraid of it happening again as you."

"I guess, but why couldn't he just tell me that, or tell me whatever it was?"

"Only he can answer that, but only if you give him that chance. Besides, makeup sex is hot, girl."

I smile. I can always count on Melissa to go down the raunchy road. She's the naughty one and I'm the romantic. It's a big part of what makes our friendship work and is one of many reasons I love this girl. I know they're right, but how the hell am I ever going to face him? Damien broke my heart into a million pieces.

It's getting late, so we divide up the rest of the pizza and wine. I help Melissa carry everything out to her car. I watch them drive away as I wait for Maggie to do her business. Once she was done, we went back inside, and I locked up, then headed to bed. I woke up the next morning drenched in sweat. What the hell, I thought, then remembered the dream I had.

In my dream, I agreed to let Damien explain. I don't remember what he said, but I remember him taking me to bed. We had the hottest makeup sex ever. I could kick Melissa's ass for putting into my head. All the dream accomplished was making me miss him and want him even more. My body was aching for his touch, but I doubted I'd ever get to feel that again.

I showered and dressed, then fed Maggie and had her do a potty break before leaving for work. I went through the motions, heart not into my work. I knew the job like I knew the back of my hand, so I could do it even while distracted. When my shift was done, I drove home, stopping on the way to grab my favorite comfort food: mint chocolate chip ice cream. I turned onto my street and saw a car parked in my driveway. There was Damien, sitting on my front porch with a bouquet in his hand.

Chapter Eight

Damien

She pulls into the driveway next to my car. I stand up and walk toward her. I hope the flowers are enough to get her to listen to me. Her face is giving nothing away, so I don't know what's about to be in store for me.

"Hi, Lexi. Did ya have a good day?"

"Up till now."

Ouch. I know I deserve that, but it still stings. I thrust the flowers in front of me.

"These are for you."

"Thanks. Is there anything else?"

"Babe, please let me explain."

"The name's Lexi, not Babe."

"Sorry. Can I please come in?"

"Nope,"

"But I'm sorry."

"Yeah, you are. Now, please leave."

Before I responded, she walked into her house and shut the door.

Well, guess the flowers weren't enough. Now what? I wish I knew how to get in touch with her friends. Though I bet they wouldn't be willing to help either. How the hell did I let this happen? I never should have fallen for her to begin with, then I freak out, and break her heart. I need my beautiful woman back in my arms.

When I get home, I give Dave his dinner, then take him over to the dog park. I keep looking for Lexi, but no sign of her tonight. After running for a while, Dave comes over and sits in front of me, his head in my lap.

"I know, buddy, I miss them, too. What am I going to do?"

He gives me the doggy head tilt, which helps improve my mood, even if it doesn't help me figure out what to do about Lexi. The rest of the week is the same. I bring Dave to the park every night, but I never see her. I can tell Dave is missing Maggie as much as I miss Lexi. The only thing taking my mind off of her besides work is my guy and I've never been happier to have him.

Saturday rolls around. After doing some work around the house, I bring Dave over to the park. I see Lexi sitting on a bench when I pull in. She looks up when she sees me, but not so much as a smile appears on her face. Of course, the minute we get inside the fence, Dave takes off and runs over to where Maggie is playing. I walk over to the bench and sit next to Lexi.

"Hi," I say. That's all you got after what you did?

"Hi," she responds, a coldness in her voice.

"Can we please talk about what happened?"

"I can't deal with this. Please, just leave me alone."

I'm about to respond, but the look on her face makes me think better of it. Instead, I nod and go find an empty bench. I glance over at Maggie and Dave. I swear they look like they're plotting something. Shit, I'm losing it. What the fuck has this woman done to me? I see Lexi grab a couple of tennis balls and walk over to the dogs. At least she's not holding my asshole behavior against Dave. I see Maggie getting tired, so Lexi picks up her toys and leashes her. Dave seems sad to see her go and comes to sit in front of me again.

"I know, boy, I'm sad to see them go, too. We'll come back tomorrow. I hope they'll be here again."

I put Dave's leash on and we walk to my car. I know what would help, but I fucked that up, so I turn around and ask Dave if he wants to take a long ride. After about 90 minutes of driving on a deserted country road, I turn around and drive back home. I stop and grab dinner at a drive-through on the way home. I feed Dave, then sit down and eat my sad excuse for a meal. I wish Lexi was sitting here with me. I wish she was naked in my bed, wrapped around my dick.

After dinner, I workout which helps me release some of my agitation. I'm still longing to have that woman in my arms, though. The light bulb goes off. I can write her a poem to get her back. I head to my music room and grab a notebook. How perfect is it that her name rhymes with sexy?

She captured my heart, my soul, my love
She came to me from the heavens above
I knew it from the start, the first time I laid eyes on her
That I wanted to love her like no other.

It's short and simple, but it's how I feel about this woman. How one person could turn my world upside down is beyond me, but damned if she didn't. Like I've done with anything else I've ever written, I put the date and time on the page, then sign it. I also put a note on why I wrote this passage. For this one, I write three words. I miss Lexi. I head off to bed after taking Dave out for his nightly business. Of course, naughty images of a certain woman fill my dreams.

Sunday brings the same old missing my woman. After my usual routine, I take Dave to the dog park. I smile and Dave wags his tail when we see Lexi playing with Maggie. As soon as I take Dave off leash, he joins in the fun. My heart skips a beat when I see Lexi laughing and smiling as she watches the dogs chase the ball. It's a beautiful East Coast spring day, blue skies and a lot of bright sun. The sun though pales compared to the beautiful face lighting up the park. The face I want to run over and kiss. Fuck, I want her back.

"Hi," I say. "I see they're having fun," nodding toward Dave and Maggie.

"They always do. I miss having fun."

Her words are like a dagger through my heart. She needs to let me back in, let me show her how much I love her. If only I could have told her. But no, I turn into a scared jackass and ruin everything.

"So, how's work been?" I ask. Lame-ass.

"Same old, same old. How about you?"

"I love being around all the old records, but it's not my dream job."

"I get that. What is your dream job?"

"I've always wanted to own a bar. A place where people could come and have a good time. I'd want to do fun stuff like karaoke and open mic nights, stuff like that."

"That sounds exciting."

"What about you?"

"I've always wanted to own a bookstore, but not just any old bookstore. I would want to combine it with food and drink, including alcohol. Similar to what you said about open mic nights, I would want up-and-coming writers, poets, even singers to have a place to showcase their talent."

I smile, thinking about how similar our dream jobs are, and how much fun it would be to combine the two. I don't want to push things as this is the most she's been willing to talk to me, but I hope to revisit this idea down the road. We spend another hour watching the dogs play.

"Maggie, come," Lexi commands.

I watch Maggie come sit in front of her. Lexi snaps on her leash, gives me a quick goodbye, then starts the walk home. A few other dogs come in and Dave runs off to play with them, so I hang out a while longer. One by one, the other dogs and their owners leave the park, until it's only me and one other guy who has a young child with him.

I see Dave run past me, full speed. I look toward the gate and see the kid opened it when his dad was tending to their dog. I yell for Dave, but he takes off out the gate. I run to my car, but he's nowhere to be found. The man is trying to apologize, but my only focus is finding Dave. I get in my car and race out of the parking lot. After an hour of driving the entire area around the park, he's nowhere to be found. I knock on doors in the area, but nobody has seen him. I keep driving for several more hours as well as checking sites on my phone where people post lost and found dogs. None of them are my Dave. I head home, distraught. I lost my woman, I can't also lose my dog.

Chapter Nine

Lexi

I t killed me seeing Damien the last couple of days. I miss him more than I realized, and Maggie has missed Dave. I sit down to have a bowl of cereal for dinner when I hear a dog barking, but not Maggie. It sounds like it's coming from outside, so I walk to my front door, Maggie hot on my heels. I look out and see Dave sitting on my front porch, but Damien isn't with him. I open the door and he comes bouncing in. I grab my cell and dial Damien's number.

"Hello," he says.

"Someone just dropped by for a visit."

"Oh my god, is Dave at your house?"

"Yeah."

"I'm on my way."

"Okay."

I hear a knock at the door. My breath catches in my throat at the thought of being alone in my house with him. I take a deep breath and answer the door.

"Dave, you crazy dog," Damien says.

Dave tears across the house and sits in front of his dad. He looks at Dave, then looks at me.

"I swear a couple of naughty dogs have been plotting this," I say.

"I'm thinking you're right."

"I would love to talk, unless you just want me to grab Dave and go."

"I'm not interested in talking. You made it clear that you no longer wanted anything to do with me."

"Babe, please."

"Lexi, please."

"Sorry."

"Never mind. Look, I'm glad Dave's okay and that he found his way here."

"Thank you for calling me."

"Of course. I can only imagine what it would have been like if Maggie went missing.

I reach down and give Dave some head rubs while Damien puts his leash on. I fight hard not to tell him to stay, but I just can't. He hurt me once and I won't let him do it again. It sure as hell is killing me, though. I want one of those romance novel moments where he grabs me and crushes his lips to mine, but this is reality and it sucks.

Monday morning arrives. I am not in the mood to deal with the dickheads who still think women shouldn't be in IT. Today will be a little bearable. My boss announced bring your dog to work day. I get Maggie ready to head into the office with me. Having her with me always calms me. When I tell her we're going for a ride, her whole backend wiggles.

I stop at Dunkin' Donuts to grab breakfast and coffee on the way to work. When we arrive, I get Maggie in her harness, grab our stuff, and walk in. Of course, she is the big hit of the day. You won't find too many breeds more beloved than a Black Lab, so she is lucky recipient of a lot of petting. I get to my desk, start up my computer, and get to work. Maggie lays there and sleeps until lunch.

I take my lunch break outside and take my girl for a walk on the campus around our building. Like any good dog mom, I have a pocket full of treats and a roll of plastic bags clipped to her leash. Of course, I need one of those bags, since her favorite thing to do is poop places she's never been. We head back in and the rest of the afternoon goes pretty fast. Maggie sleeps after her work until I tell her it's time to head home.

We stop at the dog park on the way, but no sign of Damien. I'm both relieved and disappointed. Maybe I should give in and just let him explain, but I can't bring myself to do it. I blame it on what Bryan did to me, but it sucks. For the first time in my life, I want to forget the past. I want to let Damien have his way with my body. Damn, I miss sex with him.

While I'm sitting there feeling sorry for myself, I see Melissa pull into the parking lot and smile. Hanging out with her always makes me feel better. Maggie comes running over to greet her, then goes back to playing. Melissa sits next to and puts an arm around me.

"Still no Damien I see."

"I'm trying, but I'm just not ready."

"I get it. I know how bad Bryan hurt you, but is what Damien did really that bad?"

"I thought you were on my side."

"You know I am, but I also know how happy you were. I want you to get that back."

"Sorry for snapping. I'm just a mess right now."

"Aren't we all?"

"We are."

"I gotta get going. Don't make fun, but going to try a singles mixer tonight."

"That's awesome. I hope you meet someone!"

"Me too. I need some dick bad."

We both start laughing as Melissa heads out. I toss the ball a couple more times for Maggie, then we go home to have dinner. Another night alone, wishing Damien was here. I think about what Melissa said and I know she's right. Why can't I just get over my pride and give Damien another chance? I put the TV on and Maggie jumps up next to me, her head in my lap.

"Thanks, girl," I say as I pet her head. She lets out a long, loud sigh.

"I know. I miss the guys, too. Maybe I should let Damien explain."

Maggie lets out a loud bark, making me laugh. It also helps me decide. If he tries again, I'll hear him out. After a couple hours of reading some sexy smut, I head off to bed, imagining Damien and I acting out the story I just read, and damn it was hot. We were in a very naughty club being watched while we had sex. It was by far the sexiest dream I've ever had, a credit for the amazing author who wrote the book. The rest of the week was more of the same. I hope the weekend will be better.

Chapter Ten

Damien

I can't stand one more day without her. I'm lost in thoughts of my woman as I wander through the grocery store. Suddenly, I hear a crash followed by a woman's voice.

"Watch where the fuck you're walking."

I look up and see Melissa standing there, looking pissed. I'm guessing it has very little to do with the crash.

"I'm sorry."

"Yes, you fucking are. How could you hurt someone as amazing as Lexi?"

"I know I screwed up, but if she would just let me explain. I had my heart broken bad, and I got scared."

"I get it, I do, but so did she. Then you do what you did. But for what it's worth, I tried to talk her into listening to you."

"So far, nothing has worked. Will you help me?"

"I'm only agreeing because I can see how much you love her. But you will have to embarrass yourself a bit."

"I'll do anything."

"One of her all-time favorite movies is Pretty in Pink. She loves the part where Duckie comes into the record shop, lip syncing and dancing to Otis Redding's Try a Little Tenderness."

"I've seen it. Are you sure that will work?"

"I can't make any promises, but if that doesn't work, I'm not sure anything will."

"Thank you. I mean that."

"You're welcome. And, Damien, good luck. I mean that."

Once I finish at the store, I go home, put my groceries away, and grab what I need to put my plan into action. I put Dave in the car and drive over to Lexi's house. I keep Dave on his leash next to me with ear protection on, then put Otis Redding's song on my car radio. I turn the volume all the way up and with the extra speakers I hooked up, there's no way she won't hear it.

I start lip syncing and dancing to the song in Lexi's front yard. I don't even care what I look like. All I care about is getting Lexi back. I'm only a couple of lines into the song when I see her door open. I see a smile on her face, and I smile back. I don't stop until the song ends and by the time I'm done, she's doubled over, holding her stomach. I turn and bow when I hear several of her neighbors clapping.

"Okay, you win, I'll listen," she says.

Finally. I will not screw this up again. I follow her inside. Maggie runs over, excited to see me. I take Dave off his leash and he goes to play with Maggie.

"Dave misses Maggie."

And I miss you in my arms.

"She misses him too."

I hope hers has double-meaning as well.

"Can we sit down? I need to explain."

"I guess."

"First, I need to say I'm sorry."

"Okay."

I hate her short, one-word answers, but at least she's listening to me this time. I take a deep breath and continue.

"I'd always been that man who wanted a relationship, to have the same in my arms day after day. Getting to know her, loving her, building a life with her. I thought I had found that while I was out in LA, but it was a fucking joke. When I met Brandi, she was an aspiring actress waitressing in a bar while she tried to find acting jobs.

We hit it off right away, and I fell for her. Hard. We were two years into our relationship when she got her big break. We were eating dinner when she told me. I was so excited about her news. When I jumped up to hug her, she pushed me away. She looked me dead in the face and said thank you. Only she wasn't thanking me for making her happy."

"What was she thanking you for?"

"Putting her in my music videos. I will never forget her exact words. 'I'm free of pretending to love you. I knew if you put me in enough videos, someone would notice me. I guess I should also thank you for helping me practice my acting skills.' Without another word, she turned and walked out the door."

"I'm so sorry."

"The next day, a couple of dudes showed up, packed up all her stuff, and that was that. I devastated me and broke my heart. That was started the end of my time in LA. I felt like I was choking. I dated off and on, but I was never again willing to commit, like I had to Brandi. I swore I would never let myself get hurt again, never fall in love again."

"I get it. But you could have talked to me."

"I know. I got scared."

I see a smile appearing on her face as I feel her hand on my arm. Electricity flows through my body at just that simple touch. No woman has ever affected me like her. I have to face facts. Despite my best efforts not to, I've fallen in love with this woman. I'm just not ready to tell her that yet. Nor will I ever be.

"I understand," she whispers

"So, where does this leave us?"

"You tell me."

I don't want to talk any more or I'll spill what I'm feeling in my heart for her, so I try a different approach. I throw my arms around her and kiss her beautiful mouth. Fuck, I missed tasting this woman. I feel her tongue exploring my mouth, so I twist mine around hers. I want nothing more at this moment than to be naked with her.

"Oh, Damien. Take me to bed and fuck me. Now!"

"Babe."

I follow her sexy ass to her bedroom. The second we get inside, she pawing at me, lifting my t-shirt over my head and throwing it on the floor. Her hands explore my chest as she kisses me, jamming her tongue into my mouth. I've wanted nothing as bad as I want to be inside her.

After removing her shirt and bra, I pull her in tight. Her skin against mine feels like heaven. My heart races. Damn, I'm in love with this woman and I'm not sure how much longer I can fight it. For now, though, I'm going to focus on tasting her and fucking her. I remove the rest of her clothes, then mine. I scoop her up in my arms and carry her to the bed.

We lay down together, and she's all over me. Her hands and her mouth are all over my body. I watch as she gets on all fours and slides her lips down my dick. I'm still impressed at how easily she takes my entire length down her throat. I love watching her beautiful face sliding up and down my cock while her fingers tickle my balls. She stops and looks up at me.

"I'm a naughty, naughty girl. I think I deserve a spanking."

"Fuck, babe."

She takes my dick back into her mouth. I smack her sexy bottom and feel her moan. After a couple more light smacks, I move my hand between her legs and stroke her hot pussy. I'm craving her sweet honey.

"On your back and spread those likes wide, babe."

"Mmmm, Damien."

I slide my hands under her ass and lift her hips off the bed. I bury my face between her hot legs and slide my tongue up her pussy. I swirl my tongue around her clit, making her moan.

"You taste so fuckin' sweet, babe."

"Suck me harder. Oh fuck, get rough with me. Suck my clit, oh fuck, so good."

"Damn, my naughty babe."

Her body quakes as she screams out. I lay her down as she sighs and her body relaxes.

"Mmm, Damien, so good. Now, I need to feel your dick inside me. Please, god, fuck me now. I want you so fuckin' bad."

I slide my dick in and out of her with slow thrusts. Fuck, she feels more incredible than any woman I've ever been with. She wraps her arms around me and pulls me down. Her tongue traces my lips and I kiss her hard. There's something different between us this time. It's so much more than just two people fucking. I'm making love to this woman. I give up the fight and surrender to my heart. Just the thought of loving her sends me over the edge and I empty myself deep inside her beautiful body.

I lay next to her and wrap her in my embrace, her head on my chest. She closes her eyes as I kiss her forehead.

"I love you," I said.

Her head lifts and her eyes shoot open.

Chapter Eleven

Lexi

Did he just say what I think he did?

"What?" I ask.

"Lexi, I'm in love with you."

"Oh, Damien. I'm so in love with you."

He kissed me with a tenderness I'd yet to feel from him.

"I tried to fight it. I was so afraid of getting hurt again, but babe, I just couldn't," he says.

My eyes fill up as I gaze at him. My attraction to him started the first time I saw him, but I never expected we would fall in love. Hell, I never even expected him to give me a first glance, but here we are. I can't believe I'm lying in my bed, in love, with the most incredible man I've ever known. This must be what paradise feels like.

"Are you sure about this? I can't take another heartbreak, I say."

"I've never been more sure about anything. I wanna take you out to celebrate."

I tease his chest with my fingers. "Can't we just stay in?"

"You're insatiable, babe."

"Thanks to you!"

"How about we go out to dinner, then we come back here for dessert?"

"Mmmm, that sounds perfect."

We get up and shower together. I still can't believe I'm doing this, but he makes me feel like I'm attractive. We're standing in my bedroom getting dressed when I get another surprise.

"I was thinking we should leave some stuff at each other's house," he says.

"Makes sense, especially if we're going to have more naughty sleep-overs," I say with a wink.

"How about on the way back from dinner, we stop by my house? I'll grab some stuff for me and Dave. I want to spend the night tonight, if that's okay."

"It's more than okay."

We decide on Italian for dinner. Damien ordered a bottle of my favorite wine, Moscato, and pours two glasses. He raises his glass.

"A toast to my beautiful woman. I love you."

"I'll drink to that. I love you too."

We clink glasses and each of us takes a sip. We sit and gaze at each other the whole time we're eating, like two teenagers in love. That's how he makes me feel. After we eat, Damien pays the check and we drive over to his house. He opens the door and a blur of yellow fur crashes into me.

"Hi, Dave," I say as I pet his head. "Were you trying to knock me over again?" I ask, laughing.

"He's crazy about you."

"He's awesome, just like his dad."

Once Damien has his stuff packed, we drive back to my house. Maggie and Dave wag their tails when they see each other and run off to play. We get their dinner ready, then take them for a walk. Of course, all I can think about is being back in my bed with my sexy man. Once we're inside, I grab his sexy ass.

"I believe you said something about dessert," I say.

"Go get that sexy body naked and I'll meet you in bed."

I run to my bedroom and strip, wondering what he's up to. He comes in and he's hiding something behind his back.

"Close those beautiful eyes, babe."

I hear a familiar sound I can't place at the moment, then feel something cold hitting my boobs. I then feel something cold hitting my stomach.

"Open your eyes."

I look down and whipped cream covers my boobs. Chocolate syrup covers my stomach. He runs his tongue all over my stomach until every bit of syrup is gone. He takes his tongue and swirls it around each of my boobs, licking all the whipped cream off. He kisses me hard and I can still taste the sweet cream on his tongue. I've never been as turned on as I am right now.

"I thought I was your dessert," I say, pouting.

"Babe, you are. Get those legs open so I can taste what I really want."

I brace myself for another explosion as his tongue slips inside my folds. I take flight as his tongue swipes up and down my pussy. He is so fuckin' good at this and it drives me wild. When I feel him slide a couple of fingers inside me and massage my g-spot, I lose all control. My body quakes from head to toe as I shower him with my love.

"Shit, babe, that was hot as hell. Now you get to feel my dick inside you."

"Please fuck me hard. I want you so damn much."

I feel him enter me hard and fast, taking my breath away. He's pounding me harder and faster than ever before and it feels so damn good. My entire body is bucking off the bed as I listen to him growl with every powerful thrust.

"Get ready, babe," he says as he fills me with a huge load of his salty seed. He emits one last, long growl then lays down next to me.

"Oh my god, that was incredible."

"You're incredible, babe."

"I love you."

"I love you more and I sure hope you aren't tired, as I am far from done fucking you tonight. Come be my sexy cowgirl."

I climb on top of him, sliding my body down the full length of his eager cock. I've found that I enjoy being in control like this. I angle my body for maximum stimulation as he holds me. I ride him hard and fast, feeling pleasure in places I didn't know existed until I met him. He wraps his lips around one of my boobs, sucking on my nipple. He gives it a little bite and the sting just adds to my excitement. It doesn't take me long to come undone, and I drench his cock. He keeps me there, riding him until he empties inside me and I've lost count of how many orgasms I've had.

I collapse next to him and plop my head on his chest. I'm spent, but damn, it was one hell of a ride. This man has shown me things none that have come before him ever could. He helped me realize I deserve love and that I'm not the horrible creature Bryan tried to convince me I was.

"You're quiet, you okay?" he asks.

"Got lost in thought."

"Wanna talk about it?"

"Just thinking about how much you've helped me since we met. Others have tried to tear me down, and I let them. But then here you come, and show me I'm not worthless. It's why I had such a hard time at first believing that you wanted me. I'm glad you never gave up."

"I want to kick the shit out of anyone who hurt you."

"Unnecessary, but I have to admit, I would love for some of them to see me now."

"Like this?"

I laugh. "Well, not right now."

"Good. This is just for my eyes," he says as his eyes scan the length of my naked skin.

I feel his dick stirring again. Where the hell does he keep finding all this energy? Before I'm able to ask him, I'm on my back and he's inside me. He gave me one more incredible fuck before he was spent. Neither of us had the energy for anything more than pulling the covers up and falling asleep.

Chapter Twelve

Damien

"Good morning, babe," I say when I feel her stirring beside me.

"Mmmm, good morning," she says, wiping the sleep from her eyes.

"Thank you for letting me explain."

"It was the dance that got me! But you still owe me something."

"What?"

"I told you all about my childhood."

"Yes, and you're right. How about after dinner tonight?"

"I'm holding you to that."

"You have my word. Seriously, babe, I promise I will never hurt you again."

"Good, I've had enough of that recently."

"I know, and I'm so sorry."

"But back to us. How about we save some time and shower together this morning?"

"I like the way you think."

After a hot, steamy shower together, we get dressed and each head to work. I can't wait to see her tonight, though I am a little nervous about telling her about my youth. I just hope she understands I was a different person back then. The day drags a bit, as all I want is to be with Lexi tonight. I hear a text come in on my phone.

Can't wait to see you tonight, stud.

I text her back.

I can't wait to taste you, Steamy Sugar Lips.

She responds with an eggplant and a donut.

When I'm done with my shift, I drive home and pick up Dave, then head to Lexi's house. She opens the door and I almost pass out cold. She's standing there in tight jeans and a t-shirt showing a lot of cleavage. Looking at her is making my mouth water and all I want at this moment is to get her naked. But first, I know I owe her some info. After dinner, we take Maggie and Dave for a walk, then sit down on the couch together.

"I'm as ready as I'll ever be to tell you about my youth."

"I'm sure it's not that bad."

"Promise you won't judge me."

"I promise."

"I was hell on wheels, to put it mildly. From the minute I started school, I was a troublemaker. I rarely paid attention in class and I was mouthy with the teachers. My old man held the world record for swearing, so I picked up all those words at a very young age. I knew the school principal at the elementary school I attended very well. Then I got to middle school, and I got worse. I started bullying other kids. Again, got to know the principal very well. Then something changed when I got to my last year of middle school.

The school hired a new, younger music teacher, Mr. Hyman. I'll never forget him. He was also a former rock musician, so my attitude was something he'd seen a million times. He convinced me to take music classes. It was there that I found a more creative outlet for my anger. I learned how to play guitar and drums. Then he had me try singing, and that's when I realized what I was meant to do.

Even when I moved into high school, he continued to mentor me and also became like an older brother. He was the first person to understand me and listen to me. The more I talked, the more he realized where the root of my behavior stemmed from, and he got me the help I needed. I shudder to think where I'd be today if not for him."

Looking over at Lexi for the first time since I started talking, I see tears in her eyes. Shit, I knew she was going to react like that at my being a bully. I knew I shouldn't have told her.

"It was a long time ago, babe. Please don't cry. I'm so sorry I was mean."

"That's not why I'm crying."

"What's wrong, then?"

"Why were you angry?"

"My dad. I know it sounds like a cop-out and maybe it is, but he was king of the dickheads. My mom left him when I was young and he blamed me. Knocked me around some, but more than that, it was the verbal abuse. After hearing nothing but what a loser I was, I believed him."

I feel a beautiful pair of arms wrap themselves around me and hold me tight. Her hair smells like lavender and I inhale deeply. For the first time in my life, I'm in love and I'm not scared.

"I'm so glad you found someone that helped you. Do you still keep in touch with him?"

"Mostly through text, but I would love to get the chance to see him."

"You should look him up sometime."

"I would love to take you to meet him."

"I'd love that too."

"I need to say something that may sound wimpy."

"You could never sound wimpy."

"We were made to be together, weren't we?"

"I agree. Now, I remember you texting me earlier that you wanted to taste me."

"Babe, I wanna see you strip for me."

She grabs her phone and I hear Great White's Rock Me start playing. She grinds her hips as she slowly lifts her shirt over her head, revealing a black lace bra. Holy shit! She opens the closures and runs her hands over her sexy tits and my dick stirs. She unfastens her jeans and, as she removes them, I see she's not wearing any panties.

"So fuckin' hot, babe."

She kicks off her jeans, removes her socks and shoes, then saunters over to me. My dick is practically ripping a hole in my pants after watching that. She runs her hands along my chest as she lifts and removes my shirt. I kick off my shoes and she removes my socks, her soft fingers tickling my feet. She unzips my jeans and my dick is at full attention.

"Mmmm, I'm not the only one who was going commando," Lexi says.

"Get that hot ass on the couch. NOW!"

She spreads her legs wide and I can't take my eyes off her hot pussy. Not wanting to wait another second to taste her, I run my tongue up and down her slit. I tease her clit with my tongue as she squirms.

"Tastes so sweet, babe."

"Please fuck my pussy. I need your cock inside me."

"Fuck, Lexi."

She lays down on the couch and I slide my dick inside her folds, treating her to deep, slow thrusts. Her hands find my ass and she pulls me in deeper. I wrap her in my arms as we continue this passionate dance. We move together as one, completely lost in the love we feel. I remove myself from inside her and sit down on the couch..

"Babe, come sit on my cock."

She climbs on my lap, straddling me, and takes me all the way inside her. I hold her hips as she bounces on my lap. I hear her panting as she fucks me harder. I hear her scream as her body quakes.

Chapter Thirteen

Lexi

My body is on fire as I ride wave after wave of intense pleasure. I keep bouncing hard, coming several more times, until I feel Damien fill me with his seed. I collapse against him, our chests heaving after some of the most intense sex I've ever experienced.

"Oh, Damien. Every time I think I've felt the most incredible orgasm ever, you outdo yourself. I love you."

"Babe, you make it easy. You're so damn sexy. Nothing feels more amazing that when your naked skin's against mine. I love you."

"Mmmm," I say as I shiver.

"Are you cold?"

"A little."

Damien grabs the blanket off the back of my couch and wraps it around us. I love the cozy feeling of being wrapped in his arms like this. He caresses my cheek with his hand and kisses me softly.

"I wanna take you on a date."

"We're already together."

"Yeah, but we skipped the whole date thing."

"But look at what we have done."

"The sex is incredible, babe. I just really want to do this."

"In that case, I would love to."

"Saturday night?"

"I can't wait."

Damien grabs the remote and puts the TV on. We stay cuddled under the blanket and watch a couple of shows. I can't believe I'm letting myself sit here naked like this. I don't know that I'd ever be able to explain how much this man has helped me. For the first time, well, ever, I actually like myself. He makes me feel beautiful, sexy, and desirable. I feel naughty and I slide my hand between his legs.

"You're a naughty woman."

"It's all your fault!"

"Oh, so that's how you wanna play it."

I stick my tongue out at him.

"Keep it up, babe!"

I stick my thumbs in my ears and wave my hands at him, still with my tongue sticking out. He gets up, scoops me off the couch, and carries me to bed. I try to squirm away from him, but he pulls me close.

"Oh, no you don't, woman," he says, then crushes his lips to mine, jamming his tongue in my mouth. He runs his hand down the side of my body, stopping to caress my ass as he pulls even closer. I can feel his hard cock against my mound and my pussy throbs.

"Oh god, I want you, Damien. Please, baby, fuck me hard."

"On your hands and knees, woman."

I get into position and feel him kneel behind me, his hands on my hips. With one long, hard thrust, his dick's inside me. He slides a hand around and starts teasing my clit with his fingers as he pounds into me. Suddenly, he pulls out and sits next to me.

"Baby, come to me and sit in my lap, your back against my chest."

I straddle him and grab his dick. After a couple of strokes, I take him inside me. Our bodies rock together as he fucks me. He runs his hands up my stomach as I lean back against his chest, bouncing hard on his cock as he matches me with hard thrusts. I sit up straight, taking control, my entire core on fire as his dick touches every part of my pussy.

His hands make their way to my tits, kneading them like dough as we fuck even harder and faster. Sweat pours down my body as I'm screaming.

"FUCK! So good. Oh god, DAMIEN!"

I explode around him harder than I've ever come, flooding his dick. He keeps bouncing until I feel him emptying himself inside me. I'm not even sure I can move, but he helps me lie down next to him.

"I've never done it like that before."

"I don't need to ask if you liked it."

"Just a little."

"Hey, watch using little when I'm laying here naked."

"Trust me, you're as far from little as I've ever seen. I'm naming your dick Mr. Big."

"Well, Mr. Big loves being inside that tight little pussy."

"I really wish I didn't have to go to work today."

"Me too, babe. Just wait until this weekend!"

"If I'm impressed by our date, Mr. Big will get to spend plenty of time inside that pussy."

Who the hell just said that? Holy shit, that was me. What the hell has this man done to me? I never would have the guts to say that to a guy. At least not until I met Damien.

"Well, I better plan something great."

"I promise that whatever you plan will be the best date I've ever been on."

"Dare I ask what Bryan the Dickhead did?"

"Our first date was at McDonald's. Now, had we been in high school or college, I would not have had an issue with that, but we were both working adults and both in IT, so he could have at least taken me to Applebee's or something. Truly, though, it wasn't even so much where he took me, but that he put no effort into making it special."

"I won't tell you what I have planned, but I can promise you, it will not involve McDonald's."

"Good thing or I would not have played with Mr. Big!"

His jaw drops. "Anything but that."

I walk past him, smiling and swaying my hips on my way to the shower. I feel his presence behind me, his body heat sending shivers down my spine. After a hot, steamy shower, we have a quick breakfast and take care of the dogs. I'm excited about tonight as the girls are coming over for dinner, so Mr. Sexy will have to live without me for a night. Luckily, work goes by fast.

I stop at the store to pick up food and snacks for tonight. I grab what I need, then head down to the candy aisle to grab M&Ms. We are such classy broads that we enjoy M&Ms with our wine! I head to the register and pay, then drive to the liquor store to stock up on wine for tonight. Mel's sleeping over, so we don't have to worry about how much we drink. We both scheduled tomorrow off work in order to sleep off our wine and chocolate over-indulgence. I take Maggie for a walk, then grab a shower and change into my jammies. I'm just finishing getting the food ready when I hear the door. Melissa walks into the kitchen and gives me a big hug.

While I carry the food and wine out to the living room, Melissa goes to my bedroom to get changed. Once we're all set up in the living room, we find some rom-coms to watch as we munch on snacks and kill several bottles of wine. After a few more bottles of wine, we get in our sleeping bags and pass out cold on my living room floor.

Chapter Fourteen

Damien

"Dave, come get your breakfast."

What sounds like a herd of elephants comes barreling toward me, stopping dead at his food bowl. He quickly scarfs down his kibble, then goes to the door for a potty break. I haven't been able to stop smiling since I woke up. It's finally Saturday and I have something special planned for Lexi. I've missed seeing her the last couple of days, but between her drunken girls' night and being busy with work, we haven't gotten together.

I need a few things at the grocery store, so once Dave finishes checking to see who visited the yard overnight, so I put him in the house and head out. After completing the rest of my errands, I head back home to get everything ready. I just hope she likes what I have planned.

Dave gets antsy, so I take him over to the dog park. Lexi is playing with Maggie when I get there. Dave, of course, heads right for them and starts running with Maggie. Lexi greets me with a big hug and a very sexy kiss. Mr. Big starts stirring and all I can think about is being inside her later.

"Hello, beautiful," I say when she finally removes her lips from mine.

"Mmmm, hey there, sexy."

"I can't wait until tonight, babe."

"Me either. I know it's going to be amazing."

"I don't want to give anything anyway, but I wanted to let you know to dress casual. Please don't think that means McDonald's, though."

"I know you would never to do that! I'm grateful I don't have to dress up. Not really my thing. If I could, I'd live in nothing but jeans and t-shirts."

"Especially those low-cut ones that make Mr. Big stand at full attention."

She laughs. Still one of my favorite sounds ever. Fuck, I love this woman. Maggie and Dave bark like crazy, so I look over. I nudge Lexi's arm and nod up toward the tree in the corner. We're both in hysterics watching the two knuckleheads in a staring contest with a squirrel. Lexi snorts and her face turns bright red.

"That must have been attractive," she whispers.

"Actually, it was the cutest thing I've ever heard. No need to be embarrassed."

"Glad to hear, since I do that often. I've held back laughing in front of you so I wouldn't let one slip."

"Speaking of letting things slip, let me tell you what I did once."

"Do I really want to hear this?"

"As long as you don't mind me mentioning sex with someone else."

"Not at all. I'm the one you're with now."

"So, I had just gotten to LA, a young jackass 18-year-old. The record execs threw a signing party for us and there was no lack of women. So anyway, I'm fucking this chick, totally playing the cool rockstar and my lunch choice came back to haunt me. I ripped the loudest fart in the history of forever."

"Oh, my god. I bet you both got a good laugh out of it."

"Not even close. She was so disgusted, she got dressed and ran out of the room."

"What a priss. I would have laughed my ass off. Must be all those years of watching Beavis & Butthead!"

"Holy shit, I love that show! You're the first woman I've ever met that actually admits to watching it."

"Next time we do a binge-a-thon, we're doing that show."

"I'm in. But for now, I need to get home and get everything ready. I'll be by at 6 to pick you up."

"I can't wait. Is there anything I can bring?"

"Just your appetite."

"For food or for you?"

"Both, babe."

"Yummy."

I call Dave over and, of course, his girl Maggie follows him. Lexi and I leash up the dogs and walk out to the parking lot.

"You want a lift, babe?"

"Thanks, but Maggie enjoys the walk."

I pull her in close, rubbing her sexy ass.

"See you tonight, babe."

"I can't wait."

I watch my girls leave the park and all I can think about is having that woman in my arms tonight. I want to taste her skin, taste all of her. She's mine and mine alone. Nobody will ever touch her or hurt her again.

I get home and do a quick workout, then shower and get dressed. After getting the food prepared, I pack everything up and load up my trunk. I don't want Lexi to see anything until we get to our destination. Wait until she sees the car. Nothing beats those big, roomy cars from the 50s and 60s! I saw a picture of this make, model, and year in her living room. I pack up a bag for Dave so he can stay with Maggie while we're on our date, as I plan on spending the weekend at Lexi's house.

"Dave, wanna go for a ride?"

Barking and tripping all over his own enormous paws, Dave comes running and sits down at the door. I grab his stuff and my overnight bag. I open the door and he goes right to the car and waits. The car sounds amazing when I start her up. I'm beyond excited for Lexi to see it.

"Dave, this is going to be one hell of a night for your dad. Maybe someday, Lexi will be your mom."

Holy hell, did I just say that? I've never even given a first thought to getting married and now here I am, thinking about Lexi becoming my wife. We are nowhere near that place in our relationship yet, but even the fact that I'm thinking about it and not heading for the hills is a miracle. For tonight, though, I plan on just enjoying her, making love to her. I never again want her to feel pain, or feel ashamed of herself and those sexy, sexy curves.

When we arrive at her house, I grab Dave's stuff and my overnight bag. I send Lexi a text telling her to come outside. She opens the door, and her jaw drops.

Chapter Fifteen

Lexi

A m I seeing what I think I'm seeing? No way, after all these years? Or maybe it could be. My mind is a jumbled mess as I stand frozen in place, just staring. Damien walks to my porch and lays a hand on my shoulder.

"Babe, I knew you would love this car after I saw that picture in your living room."

"Where did you get this?"

"I found it for sale a couple of towns over."

"Can I look in the glove box?"

"Sure."

"Oh, my god. Come look."

"Babe, that's your name!"

I throw my arms around Damien. I can't believe he found it. Destiny sent this man to become part of my life, but I never would have expected this to be the reason.

"Let's get the dogs settled and I'll tell you all about on our way to our date."

"Can't wait."

Damien and I feed the dogs, put them out for a potty break, then head out for our date. Damien won't give me any clues about our date, which makes me even more excited. Once we're on the road, I tell him about the car.

"You don't know just how amazing it is that you found this car. My pop-pop owned this car. He told me it would be mine someday, but he never put that in his will. When he passed away, my dad didn't honor his wishes and sold the car. HIm selling the car devastated me, not because of the monetary value, but because it was so special to me.

My parents never got me, but pop-pop did. I spent a lot of time hanging out with him. He taught me how to drive in this car. Losing him was one of the hardest things I ever had to go through, so watching someone else drive away in that car broke my heart. I never thought I would see it again. I love that I get to ride in it again."

"Thank you for sharing that with me. I can't believe I found it."

"What was meant to be was that I found you. I love you."

"I love you, babe."

We reach our destination and Damien pulls into a wooded area. We exit the car and he walks around to the trunk. He grabs a couple bags and a guitar case, along with a cooler. He leads me a little way into the woods to a clearing. The weather is beautiful tonight, a perfect warm spring evening. Damien lays a blanket on the ground.

"Come join me, babe."

I walk over to the blanket and he helps me sit. He joins me and opens the cooler. Inside I see a bottle of champagne and two glasses. The cooler also has a small container of strawberries, and some other bags of food.

"I saw you had a well-worn copy of Pretty Woman near your TV."

He pops the champagne and pours two glasses. After handing me a glass, he raises the other.

"A toast to the best date ever," he says.

"I'll drink to that."

After we clink glasses, we each take a sip, then each eat a strawberry. He opens one of the bags and pulls out two paper plates and a box of crackers. He takes a bag of cheese out of the cooler and we each make a plate. After we finish eating and finishing our champagne, Damien grabs his phone and turns some music on. He stands and helps me up.

"Please dance with me, babe."

"I'd love to."

He wraps his around me and pulls me close, as I circle mine around his neck. We sway together to the music. He leans down and crushes his lips to mine, jamming his tongue into my mouth. We dance and kiss our way through several songs before he peels himself away.

"Come lay with me, babe."

We lay down on the blanket and he kisses me even harder. His hands slip under my shirt as he lifts it, exposing my stomach. His lips caress my skin and I feel a dampness between my legs. He lifts my shirt off and removes my bra. His sexy mouth and tongue work their magic on my breasts as I writhe beneath him.

He takes my sneakers and socks off, then opens my jeans. I lift my bottom and he slides them down. He hooks his fingers on my panties and slides them down. He looks me up and down, a wicked smile on his face.

"Babe, you're the most beautiful woman I've ever seen. I want nothing more than to taste you. Spread those pretty legs for me."

He kisses and sucks on my neck. His tongue slides down between my breasts and down my body until he reaches my pussy. I'm so hot for him at this point that even the slightest touch of his tongue drives me wild. Instead of putting his tongue where I want it most, he opens the cooler and grabs an ice cube. Holding the ice cube in his hand, he let it drip down my body.

He moves his hand lower and opens my folds with his other hand. He lets the ice cube drip onto my open pussy, sending shivers down my spine. He puts the ice cube in his mouth and starts licking my pussy. Damien combining his hot tongue and the cold ice is sending me into space.

"Oh, Damien, that feels so good, baby."

He doesn't answer, as his tongue is too busy pleasuring my pussy. My body is on fire as I quiver. I'm approaching orgasm, thanks to that sexy man.

"Oh, baby, I'm so close. Please suck my clit."

With the ice still in his mouth he sucks my clit hard, the sensation sending me over the edge and I explode all over his face.

"OH. FUCK. DAMIEN!"

"How did that feel, babe?"

"So incredible. I've had no one use ice quite like that. I hope you plan on doing that again sometime."

"Oh, yes, babe. But right now, I don't want anything except to be inside you."

"Please baby, I wanna feel your dick inside me."

Chapter Sixteen

Damien

I grab her Lexi's hot legs and lift them. She looks so damn sexy, legs spread up in the air. I lower my body on top of her and slide my dick deep inside her. She wraps her legs around my waist, keeping me pressed tight against her. Her hands make their way to my ass as I fuck that sweet pussy. Nothing feels better than being with her like this, especially outside like animals.

"Fuck, babe, you feel so damn good. I can't get enough of that hot pussy."

"So good, oh Damien, I wanna feel you come inside me. Please fuck me hard."

I slam into her hard and fast, my balls slapping that sweet ass with every thrust. Fuck, this woman unleashes the beast inside me. I can't take it anymore and I empty inside her, groaning as I give her a couple more quick thrusts before I lay down next to her. I pull her into my arms, then grab another blanket to cover us. Lexi lays her head on my chest and looks up at me with her beautiful emerald eyes.

"I've never done it outside before. Nobody's ever used an ice cube on me before. I can only imagine what other new things you still have to teach me."

"Babe, there is. You just have to let me know what your limits are."

"How do I know? There's so much I've never done."

"We'll need to talk first. I will never do something you're uncomfortable with."

"Mmmm, I'm excited."

I hear rustling in the woods. Suddenly, a man and woman appear near where we're laying. They see us and smile.

"Holy shit, you're Mikael Andersson."

"Guilty. This is my wife, Hannah."

"Umm, this is my girlfriend, Lexi."

"No need to be embarrassed. We've done it outside on more than one occasion."

"Thanks," I say.

"We saw a couple other cars pull in, so you should get dressed," Hannah says.

"Appreciate it," I say.

"We'll be on our way to give you two some privacy."

"That's certainly now how I wanted to meet him," Lexi says.

"I guess not, but at least they were cool about it."

"Definitely."

We heed their warning and get dressed, then sit back down on the blanket. Not exactly my plan, but this won't ruin what else I have in store for my babe. I grab my guitar and take it out of the case. Lexi's face lights up when she sees it.

"Any requests, babe?"

"Surprise me."

I decide to go with super-romantic 'What Love Can Be' by Kingdom Come. She sits between my legs, her back against my chest. I hold the guitar in front of her and start strumming, singing the beautiful words to her. I'm about halfway through the song when Mikael and Hannah come by again.

"Apologies for interrupting, but you're really talented," Mikael says.

"Thanks, man. I used to be in a band way back, but the scene was too much for me. I ended up leaving LA and moving here."

"Sounds familiar," Hannah says.

"How so?" Lexi asks.

"That's how we met. Mikael first came here to attend a friend's wedding. We met and became friends who eventually fell in love and got married."

"Wow, that's so cool," Lexi says.

"How did you two meet?" Mikael asks.

"My dog kinda knocked her on her butt."

Hannah and Mikael both laughed.

"That sounds like one of those romance novels 'meet-cutes' I love reading," Hannah says.

"Sweetie, I think we've interrupted these two enough," Mikael says. "Besides, I suddenly have the urge to get you home."

"Oh Mikael, you are insatiable."

We all laugh as they wave and head off. I resume singing to Lexi, loving the way she feels against me while I play for her. I look at her and see that her eyes are closed and she has a dreamy look on her beautiful face. I finish the current song and whisper in her ear.

"I love you, babe."

"I love you too, Damien."

"Babe, we need to go home now!"

"Yes we do. I want you bad."

She helps me clean up and carry everything back to the car. Fuck, I can't wait to get her home and get her naked. I turn the radio on in the car and find an oldies station. We sang at the top of our lungs for the entire ride home. This is the first time I've heard Lexi sing, and holy shit, she's incredible. Why has she never shared this gift with anyone?

"Babe, you told me you have no musical talent, but you're an amazing singer."

"Oh, yeah right. I'm already sleeping with you. No need to flatter me."

"Trust me, I'm not. I've never heard a voice quite like yours. You need to stop hiding your gift."

"Are you serious?"

"Babe. You need to sign up for an open mic night at the club."

"I would never have the guts to do that."

"What if I was up there with you? We could sing a duet or I could play guitar for you."

"I don't know."

"Promise me you'll think about it."

"Okay, that I can agree to."

I am going to get that woman on that stage. Everyone needs to hear that voice. I think about what she could sing and the perfect song plays on the radio.

"That's it!"

"What's it?" she asks.

"I know what you should be singing. This would be perfect."

"No way. I could never do Janis justice. She is incredible."

"You're wrong. You're incredible. You need to get up on that stage and sing Me and Bobby McGee."

She's quiet for a minute, then belts out the song and holy shit. I'm blown away. I'm pissed that nobody ever told her she could sing. I cannot wait for the world to hear this woman, MY woman, up on that stage singing her heart out. Time for to download some sheet music and learn that song. We pull into her driveway and I shut off the car. I'm about to get out, but she stops me.

"Before we go inside, I need to say something."

"What's up, babe?"

"Thank you for tonight. I knew this was going to be the best date I've ever been on, but I didn't know just how great. I've never made love outside before and holy shit, that ice. And then to be treated to you singing and playing for me. I'm not sure what I did to deserve to meet someone like you, but I'm grateful. Being knocked on my ass by Dave was the best thing that could have happened to me. I'm completely in love with you."

"Babe, this was the most fun I've ever had on a date. I love how open you are to everything. I've had more fun with you than with anyone in my life. Not are you beautiful and sexy as hell, you're also funny and someone I can not only be lovers with but also someone I can be friends with. That is one thing that's always been missing with any other relationships I've been in. I love you more than I ever knew it was possible. Let's go inside so I can show you just how much."

Chapter Seventeen

Lexi

"Oh, Damien, you need a shave and a breath mint."

I sit up with a start, remembering the strange dream I just had. When I see who's in the bed with me, the dream makes more sense. I'm surrounded by two furry bedmates, but my sexy man is nowhere to be found. My nose tells me why. I'm naked. No surprise after the night we had, so I get up and put my robe on. I walk out to the kitchen, two dogs hot on my heels.

"Good morning, babe. Hope you want some breakfast."

"I see what I want."

Damien is standing there wearing nothing but an apron. I can't take my eyes off him. While Maggie and Dave drool over the plate of bacon on the counter, I'm drooling over his sexy, naked ass. I walk over and run my hand over his ass.

"Fuck, woman, are you trying to awaken Mr. Big?"

"I could go for some sausage."

"Damn, woman, you didn't have enough last night?"

"Is there a such thing?"

"Just you wait. For now, though, breakfast is served."

I watch as my sexy naked chef serves me an omelet with a side of bacon and rye toast, along with a cup of coffee. The food is delicious but what I want in my mouth is hiding under that apron. I intend to have some of that after breakfast. I find it impossible to take my eyes off my sexy man. Once we're done eating and cleaning up, I walk over to the counter where Damien is standing and put my hand under the apron.

"Hey, naughty woman."

"I want you, my sexy man."

I get down on my knees, put my head under the apron, and wrap my lips around his erection. As I'm sliding my mouth up and down his dick as I tease his balls with my fingers. I look up and see him throw his head back, growling as I suck on him.

"Oh, fuck, Lexi, so good, babe."

I don't answer, my mouth otherwise occupied, and start sucking harder. He tastes so damn good. I love feeling him come in my mouth, so I keep increasing the pressure of my lips on his dick. I hear his breathing get shallow. It won't be long now and I'll get to drink him down.

"Fuck, babe, I'm coming. Holy fuckin' shit, woman."

I feel a huge load of his warm cream in my mouth. Looking up into his gorgeous brown eyes, I swallow every drop and lick my lips.

"Get that hot ass on the counter. Now, babe."

He helps me up onto the counter and spreads my legs.

"So fuckin' pretty," he says, staring between my thighs. "Hold on tight, woman."

"Oh, Damien."

"Are you still interested in trying something new?"

"Oh, yes, my sexy man."

"Good. Wait right here."

Damien goes to where his overnight bag is sitting. He comes back with a feather in his hand and something hidden behind his back in his other hand. He walks back over to me and kisses me hard.

"Babe, do you trust me?"

"Mmm, yes."

"I want to blindfold you, but only with your consent."

"Yes, please, baby."

He slips the blindfold over my eyes and I can't see anything. I feel an excitement building in my stomach.

"Now, I want to be in charge. If you agree, you have to do everything I tell you."

"I want this."

"Good girl. Spread those legs as wide as you can. Good. Now, I want to watch you pleasure yourself. Get those fingers to work, woman."

I'm turned on by the thought of him watching me. Before I met him, I would have died at the thought of someone seeing this. I decide to tease him a bit, so I slide my finger in my mouth before I tease my pussy.

"So fuckin' sexy, babe. Let me see you rubbing that hot clit. And I better enjoy it or I put Mr. Big away."

I giggle a little, then stroke my clit. I throw my head back and moan. If there's one thing I'm good at, it's taking care of my own needs. I've had plenty of practice. I wonder what my sexy man thinks of this, and I wish I could see his face.

"Mmm, babe, that was so hot, but you can stop now. I want you to taste yourself.."

I slide my finger inside my mouth, and I'm surprised at first, but I like it.

"I'm pleased, so you get a reward."

He opens my pussy with his strong fingers and I feel the feather sweeping along my clit. My body shivers at the sensation. I hear a buzzing sound and feel a vibrator between my legs. Damien turns the power all the way up, and the sensation is almost more than I can handle.

"Oh, Damien, so good."

"Better than me?"

"Oh, baby, nothing feels better than you."

"What do you want in your pussy?"

"Please, Damien, please fuck me with that incredible cock."

"Where do you want it?"

"Right here on the counter."

"Good answer, woman."

71

I'm still blindfolded, so I can't see where Damien is. I gasp when I feel his monumental cock enter me. I wrap my legs around his waist as he fucks me. I can feel his breath on me, hear his breathing get shallow as he fucks me hard. I love everything about this man. Raking my nails along his back makes him growl even louder.

"OH. FUCK. LEXI."

He comes inside me hard. His body bucks as he finishes emptying himself deep inside me.

"Babe, keep those legs wrapped around me and put your arms around my neck."

I do as I'm told. He lifts me off the counter and starts walking. I can't see, so I'm not sure where he's taking me. I feel my bed beneath me.

"I'm going to remove your blindfold. Close your eyes so the light doesn't hurt."

He lays down next to me and pulls me close.

"Tell me how that felt, babe."

"It felt so naughty. I loved being blindfolded. I was a little nervous when you asked me to touch myself, but I enjoyed knowing that you were watching me. I can't believe all the stuff I've done with you. Even the thought of someone seeing without clothes scared the hell out of me."

"Babe, I know I've told you this before, but I never want you to forget it. You're are by far the sexiest, most beautiful woman I've ever known. And that beauty is so much more than what you look like. When I see you with you with Maggie and now also with Dave, it warms my heart. Now, I need you to do something for me tonight. And before you say no, think about everything else you've done."

"Uh oh."

Chapter Eighteen

Damien

Now's my chance. I'm determined to get her to sing, and the club is having an open mic night tonight. Why am I nervous? I know she's resistant to this, but the woman is an amazing singer and the world needs to hear her. Time to turn on the charm.

"You feel like going out tonight?"

"What'd you have in mind?"

"How about the club?"

"I'd love to. I thought you were going to ask me for something difficult. I was worried about nothing."

"Full disclosure. Going to the club is not my only request. Babe, please hear me out. When I heard you sing, I got chills. I'm not just saying that because I love you. I've heard a lot of singers and nobody has ever affected me the way you did. You need to share that gift."

"I just can't. I'm sorry."

"Why not? What are you afraid of?"

"How can I get up onstage looking like this? People are going to either laugh at me or boo me off the stage."

"Babe, that will not happen. Please, look at all the stuff you've done with me you never thought you would. What do I have to do to convince you to do this?"

"Okay, if you want me to do this, you have to do something first."

"What babe?"

"Go outside and do one lap around my house."

"That's it?"

I get up and start getting dressed.

"Oh, no you don't. You need to go just as you are right now."

"Babe, I'm naked."

"I'm aware."

"So that's how you want to play. Fine. If I do this, you promise you'll sing tonight?"

"Well, one more thing."

"What?"

"You'll be on stage with me playing."

"Of course."

I get up and walk out to Lexi's living room. She puts a robe on and follows me. I can't believe I'm doing this, but if this is what it takes to get her to sing tonight, I'll do it. Just as I open her front door, I see Melissa pull into her driveway. Her eyes go wide when she sees me. I see her walk over to stand with Lexi on the porch.

As I start my lap, I hear Melissa say, "Damn girl, you must have fun in bed with him. He's huge."

As I run, I'm aware of my dick being out for all the world to see, well at least Lexi's neighbors. As I'm coming back, I hear whistles and catcalls as Melissa and Lexi are standing there with goofy grins on their faces. I will never live this down, but it was worth it.

"I'm guessing there's a story behind what I just witnessed, but I'll save that for our next girl's night," Melissa says. "I'll just say, quite impressive."

Lexi's cheeks redden as I respond. "Thank you. But I do believe I should get inside before anyone calls the police."

I stand inside her front door and hear Melissa say, "Get your cute ass in the house and play with that sexy hunk."

She hugs Lexi goodbye and drives away. Lexi walks inside, a wicked look on her face.

"That was so fuckin' hot. You must want me to sing tonight."

"I do, babe. I hope you believe me now that I think you're amazing. I would never have done something like that unless I believed in your talent. I can't wait until tonight. I have one more surprise for the performance."

"What's that?"

"I want you to pick which of my guitars I play tonight."

"Okay."

"How about we take the dogs to the park for a while, then we can go over my house and check out my collection?"

"That sounds fun. I'll even let you put clothes on this time."

After a sexy shower, we get dressed, pack up toys and water for Maggie and Dave, then drive to the dog park. After an hour of running, the dogs are exhausted, so we take them to my house. When we get inside, both dogs lie together in the living room. I walk over to my basement door.

"Ready to go check out my guitars?"

"Yes, let's go!"

"Have a seat on the couch, babe."

After the sits, I lift the cover off my collection. Lexi's eyes go right to my purple guitar. It's my favorite, so I'm hoping that's the one she picks.

"So, what do you think?"

"The purple one is my favorite."

"Mine too."

I pull the purple guitar off the rack and put it in a case, then put the cover back on. I walk over and sit next to Lexi.

"I'm scared," she whispers.

"I understand. It took a long time before I was comfortable on stage. I promise it will get easier each time you do it. And remember, I'll be right there with you."

"Thank you."

"I love you, babe. Now, I want to help you relax."

"Mmm, okay."

I walk behind the couch and start massaging her shoulders. I feel the tension leave her body and she sighs. I suck on the back of her neck and she moans.

"Is there anything you aren't good at?"

"Lots of things."

"I've yet to see any."

"I hope you never do."

I don't need for her to know some things I've done in my past. I hate hiding things from her. I can't mess this up, so for now, I keep some of my past to myself. For now, my focus is getting her through what I hope is the first of many performances.

"Is there anything else you need to do to get ready for tonight, or do you want to feed the dogs and walk them before we go?"

"As long as you think I'm dressed okay, I don't need to do anything else."

"You look like a sexy rocker chick to me, babe."

"Then let's get the dogs taken care of."

Lexi and I head upstairs and get Maggie and Dave fed, then take them for a quick walk around my neighborhood. We grab a quick bite, then head over to the club. I can't wait to see everyone's reaction when they hear her sing. I hope her friends are there tonight. I thought about inviting them, but I want them to be surprised by her talent. She deserves this after the way people have treated her.

We arrive a little while later and I let Doug know we will both be on stage, but ask him to only introduce me. I smile when I see Melissa show up a little while later, and I can't wait to see her face. Lexi and I are waiting side-stage when we see Doug walk out and grab the microphone.

"Welcome to open mic night, everyone. We have a special treat kicking us off tonight. Put your hands together for Damien St. James."

I wait until I see Doug nod, then I approach the mic.

"Thanks, Doug. I have an extra special performance planned. So extra special that I can't do it alone. Let's get another round of applause going for Lexi Carter."

I see Melissa's jaws drop, then turn to watch Lexi walk on stage. I give her a smile and a wink when she walks past me and she smiles back. I watch her walk up to the mic and I've never been more excited. She sings, and my heart skips a beat. She sounds even better than she did in the car. By the end of the song, she's belting it out and when she finished and bows, she's met with a standing ovation. Melissa has a huge smile on her face, tears streaming down her face. I walk over, grab Lexi's hand and we walk off stage together.

Chapter Nineteen

Lexi

Damien and I get backstage. I can still hear the crowd roaring. I'm still in disbelief that I did that.

"They loved you. Listen to that crowd," I say.

"Babe, that's for you. I thought you sounded great in the car, but what I just heard was incredible. I'm so damn proud of you, not just for being amazing, but for having the courage to do it."

I'm about to respond when the dressing room door bursts open and I find myself in the middle of a friend sandwich.

"Damn, girl, how come we never heard you sing before," Melissa says.

I shrug my shoulders, feeling uncomfortable at all the attention.

"She's amazing, but it took some convincing to get her to do this," Damien says.

Melissa gasps and covers her mouth with her hand.

"Is that what the naked lap was for?" Melissa asks.

"Yep. I told him that was the only way I would perform," Lexi says.

"Damn, my friend's a badass," Melissa teases.

This was an enormous step for me, and I want to keep feeling good about it. I walk next to Damien and feel his arms wrap around me. Melissa gets in on the hug before she heads out.

"I would love to stay and celebrate, but I need to be up early in the morning," Melissa says.

"I'm so glad you were here tonight."

"Me too. You kicked ass, girl. That better not be the last time I get to hear you sing."

"It won't," Damien answers.

"Night girl."

I take a seat on the couch and Damien joins me. He puts a hand under my chin and tilts my head up.

"The crowd loved you. Melissa was right. You kicked ass up there."

I'm about to respond when I hear a knock on the dressing room door. Damien walks over and answers it. I look over and see Doug walking in with Damien.

"Lexi, you brought the house down tonight. I lost count of how many people stopped by the bar to ask if you would perform again. I sure hope it will be soon."

"I was expecting to be booed off the stage."

"Babe, stop that."

"I agree with Damien. I hope there were people we went to school with in that crowd so they could see how wrong they were about you," Doug says. "You're both welcome to perform at any time."

"Thanks, man," Damien says.

When Doug leaves, Damien returns to the couch.

"What did Doug mean?"

"You know how they have all those 'most likely to succeed' type things? Well, the other students made up some of those that weren't included in the yearbook. They named me least likely to amount to anything and least likely to lose my virginity."

"Fuckers. If only they could see you now."

"They could, but I'm not going."

"Going where?"

"I got a notice the other day that my 30th reunion is coming up."

"Babe, we're going."

"No way."

"Yes way. I'll do two naked laps if I need to. You need to show those fuckers what they were missing out on."

"I'll think about it."

"Good. Now, let's stop by the diner and grab a quick bite before we head home."

"Damien."

"What, babe?"

"Thanks for making me do this."

"Of course, babe. I love you."

"Mmmm, love you so much."

Damien drives us to the diner, where we indulge in pancakes and hot chocolate with loads of whipped cream. In a moment of silliness, I take a finger-full and put it on his nose. He licks it off with that sexy tongue of his.

"You're in so much trouble when we get home."

"Promise?"

"Babe, you looked like a total rockstar up on that stage tonight. I get to be your groupie."

"And what do you want to do with the hot rocker chick?"

"I want to fuck her brains out."

"Then get your ass into the bedroom and wait for my instructions."

"Excuse me?"

"I'm the rockstar. You're just a groupie, so you have to do what I tell you.

"And if I don't?"

"Then no pussy for you tonight."

"Babe."

I sit on the bed, grab my phone, and play Poison's Talk Dirty to Me.

"Strip for me. And I damn well better enjoy the show."

I watch Damien remove his clothes, feeling a dampness between my legs. I want him so fucking bad, but I'm not telling him that. He stands there naked in front of me as my eyes travel the length of his chiseled body. He's so damn hot. I want to jump him now, but he has to earn it first.

"Good. Now, grab that cock and stroke it for me, baby."

"Damn, woman."

"I wanna hear you enjoy it."

He strokes his cock and groans as I remove my shirt and bra. I grab my breasts and lick my lips. He responds by stroking himself harder. Good, I'm driving him wild. But, he hasn't seen anything yet. I remove the rest of my clothes and sit back down. I spread my legs wide so he can see what he wants most. He strokes harder and throws his head back.

"Look at me."

He looks and his jaw drops when he sees me with two fingers inside my pussy. My other hand strokes my clit as he watches. I want to tease him, but my pussy throbs hard and I need him to fuck me now.

"Come to me, my sexy man."

I smile as he walks over, dick rock hard. I take a finger and wipe the pre-cum from his dick. I slide my finger in my mouth, savoring his taste. He growls like a bear. I lay back.

"I want your dick inside me now. I want you to fuck me hard and fast, like the fucking animal you are."

"Fuck, you hot sexy woman."

He grabs my leg and lifts it in the air. With one hard thrust, he fills my pussy with his cock and pounds me hard and fast. It feels so fucking good and I lose all control. I assail his ears with a stream of dirty words that would make a sailor blush. I'm not sure, but I may have invented some new ones.

"Sit up and wrap those legs around my waist, babe."

I grab his ass, pulling him in deeper as he fucks me so hard, I bounce on and off the bed. The headboard bangs into the wall so hard, the dogs start barking. I hear Damien emit a long, low growl as I feel him fill me.

"Fuck, woman, so good. Your turn now."

He takes his fingers and spreads my pussy wide. He strokes my pussy hard, and I quickly come undone, screaming at the top of my lungs. My body shakes from head to toe as I ride waves of incredible pleasure.

"Holy. Fucking. Shit. I need to sing more often."

We're lying in my bed, holding each other, basking in the afterglow of some heated passion.

"I wanna have a party to celebrate your debut. How about next

Saturday night at my house? It's warm enough that we could do it outside."

"I'm up for a party, but only if you let me help plan things."

"I want to do this together, babe."

"I was thinking about something you said. Are you still willing to go to my reunion with me?"

"Damn right. I want to see everyone's faces when you walk in."

"Then I'm sending the paper in and we're going."

"That's my badass chick!"

"None of this would have happened to me if not for you."

"That's where you're wrong, babe. I may have helped you find your strength, but there had to be something to find."

"I never thought of myself as strong, especially with how quiet I am."

"Volume doesn't equal strength. In my experience, the ones who yell the loudest are the weakest. They use that volume to trick people, and themselves, into believing they're strong."

"I imagine you ran into many people like that in LA."

"More than I care to remember. It's one of many reasons I needed to get away from that scene. When I first moved here, I wasn't sure I'd made the right decision. Then Dave knocks this woman on her ass and I realize this is where I belong."

"For sure, I'm grateful you made that move. Otherwise, all my orgasms would still be from my Bob!"

"Who's Bob? You never mentioned any men other than Bryan."

I can't even pretend to control my laughter and let loose the loudest snort ever.

"Bob stands for battery-operated boyfriend, silly."

Damien joins me in laughter until we're both sitting there with tears streaming down our faces.

"Who's better, me or Bob?"

"You. I would rather have a warm dick inside me any day. Especially when that dick belongs to someone as special as you."

"Babe, let's get that dick inside you now!"

Chapter Twenty

Damien

After one more hot and heavy fuck, we get some sleep. Lexi leaves Maggie here to be with Dave all day. I want her to move in, but I'm afraid to bring it up. I don't want to scare her if she thinks it's too soon. We head to our cars to leave for work and see Judd taking care of his horses.

"Good morning, Damien. Good morning, Miss Lexi," he says.

Lexi and I answer, "Good morning," in unison. I take her hand as we walk to our cars. I give her a big hug and a passionate kiss, guaranteed to keep her wet all day.

"I love you," she says, then gets in her car and starts it up, the sound of David Coverdale's voice filling the air.

"Love you too, babe."

She waves, then pulls out of the driveway. I miss her as soon as she's gone. I've said it before, but no woman has ever affected me quite like my babe. The alphahole I was in my twenties would never act like this, but at this phase of my life, the only thing I want is one woman to spend the rest of my life with, and I know for sure, Lexi is that woman. I can't get my mind off her my entire drive to work. When I get inside, I see Mikael standing there talking to Kurt. He smirks when he sees me.

"Well, well, if it isn't the naked guitarist!" Mikael teases. "Hey, Hannah, come see who's here."

"I remember you. Where's that cute girlfriend?" Hannah says.

"Do I want to hear this story?" Kurt asks.

"The other night, I took my girl, Lexi, on a date. We were having a picnic in the woods and, well, things got heated. After we were done, I wrapped us in a blanket and I was singing to her. We heard rustling, and it turned out to be Mikael and Hannah. They were kind enough to warn us that others were heading our way, so we could get dressed."

"That must have been a fun date," Kurt said.

"It was! I love that woman," I replied.

"I'll never understand why," I hear behind me.

"I beg your pardon. Who the hell are you," I say to the rude blonde woman.

"I'm Amy and I went to school with Lexi. Men are supposed to love women who look like me, not her."

"I'm going to refrain from any comments while I'm at work. However, I need to walk away before that changes," I say after a couple of deep breaths.

"I appreciate my employee's professionalism. As store co-owner, however, I am exercising my right to refuse service to you. Please remove yourself from the premises and don't return," Hannah said.

Amy turned to leave, but before she walked out the door, she looked back at me and said, "This isn't over."

"What the hell?" Mikael said.

"This reminds me of something that happened to my friend Alex," Hannah added. "Might I offer some advice?"

"Please," I say.

"I know it's going to hurt her, but you need to tell Lexi what happened. I promise you, it will be worse if she finds out you knew and kept it from her."

"I understand. My first thought was not to tell her, but I know I need to. Thank you and please accept my apology for what happened."

"Let me walk you over to the record store," Hannah says.

When we get to the other part of the store, Hannah comes behind the counter with me.

"Alex went through something similar with a couple of her friends. A couple of her friends got jealous, and they turned on her, said some horrible things. Hearing Amy just now reminded me of that. Even though Amy's not her friend, expect that she will be upset when you tell her and just be there for her."

"Thank you for the advice, not my area of expertise."

"We women are complicated creatures."

"Yeah, but worth it."

"Yes we are. It took Mikael's love to show me that."

Hannah's cell rings, so she excuses herself and returns a couple of minutes later.

"That was Cherie. She's not feeling well this morning. Are you fine handling things on your own today?"

"She taught me well. Hope she feels better."

"Thanks. If you need anything, just let Kurt know."

"Will do."

The store was a little busier today, but nothing I can't handle. I'm dreading what I have to do later. The last thing I want is to hurt or upset Lexi. I'm lost in thought when I hear the shop door open. I look up and see Melissa walk in.

"Hey there," she says when she approached the counter.

"Good afternoon. May I help you?"

"Do you have a few minutes to chat?"

"Sure, but if a customer comes in, I'll need to take care of them."

"Got it. I ran into an old classmate, Amy, at the grocery store and she had nothing nice to say about you."

"Not surprised. She came in here insulting Lexi, so Hannah kicked her out. Now, I get to home tonight and tell her."

"What did she say?"

"That men are supposed to love women that look like her, not like Lexi."

"Bitch."

"My thought as well. How am I supposed to tell Lexi? It's going to crush her."

"How about if we tell her together?"

"Are you sure? I hate to put anyone else in that position."

"I love that girl, so please let me help."

"One more thing. Before she left, she said this wasn't over. Any idea what else she might do?"

"No, and that has me worried."

"Same. I won't stand for anyone hurting my girl."

"I'm glad she found you. She deserves so much happiness. I gotta run, but what time should I stop over?"

"Does six work?"

"I'll be there."

"Thanks, Melissa."

The rest of the day went by pretty fast. When I pull into my driveway, Lexi's waiting on my porch.

"How was your day, babe?"

"Not too bad. Yours?"

"Same."

"You sure you're okay?"

"All good, babe. You know, it just occurred to me I should give you a key."

"Oh."

"That way you can let the dogs out to potty."

"Oh, that makes sense then."

Shit, I almost fucked that up. I really want her to live here with me, but I'll have to wait for now. After we eat dinner, we feed the dogs and take them outside to play. I'm dreading what I have to do, but glad Melissa will be here to help. A little before six, I hear a knock on the door.

"Can you wait with the dogs while I see who that is?" I ask.

"Of course."

Melissa follows me to the backyard and sits down at the table with Lexi. I'm too nervous so I stand and pace. I see Lexi looking back and forth between Melissa and me, so I take a deep breath and start.

"Babe, I need to talk to you about your old classmate, Amy. That's why Melissa's here."

"What the hell's going on?"

"Amy came into the record store today when I was talking with Kurt, Mikael, and Hannah. I was talking about how much I love you and I heard a voice behind me. She said she couldn't understand why and that men were supposed to love women that look like her and not you. I kept my cool since I was at work, but Hannah immediately threw her out. Before she left, she turned back to me and told me it wasn't over."

"I had stopped by the store to talk to Damien after I ran into Amy at the grocery store and she was bad-mouthing Damien. He told me what happened, so we wanted to tell you together what happened," Melissa added.

Lexi's reaction sure wasn't what I expected. She stood up, hands balled into fists, her face the brightest crimson I'd ever seen.

Chapter Twenty-One

Lexi

"That skinny, flat-chested bitch. She can kiss my fuckin' ass."

Melissa just sits there, mouth wide open, but nothing coming out. This may be the first time in history she's ever been silent.

"Damn, woman. Not at all what I was expecting."

"Let me guess, you expected me to cry. That's the old Lexi, but you, my sexy man, have awakened a beast and the fuck if anyone is putting her back to sleep."

After she recovers, Melissa stands and bows down at me. "Damn, girl, this is the badass I always knew was in there. Thank you, Damien, for bringing her to life."

"My pleasure," he says, a wicked grin on his face.

"Mine too," I say.

Melissa's jaw drops again. I wonder what that's all about.

"Hey ya'll. Nice night tonight."

Oh, that's why, I think to myself, wheels spinning.

"Would you like to join us, Judd?" I ask.

Damien shoots me a look that tells me he knows what I'm thinking.

"Howdy, ma'am," he says to Melissa.

She giggles like a schoolgirl, unable to speak.

"Judd, this is my best friend, Melissa. Melissa, this is Judd Walker."

"A pleasure," Judd says as he takes Melissa's hand and kisses it.

She giggles again, but at least manages a hello this time.

"Can I get you something to drink?" I ask Judd.

"Beer, please,"

"Coming right up. Mel, do you wanna help me?"

Melissa jumps up and follows me inside.

"Holy shit, he's hot," Melissa says, fanning herself.

"I knew the first time I saw him you'd like him. I know your type. Think you can handle giving him his beer?"

"I'll try."

"Remember your words," I tease.

"Shut it, bitch!"

We return to the guys. We're both in hysterics.

"That can't be good," Damien jokes.

Melissa puts the beer down in front of Judd, but again no words come out.

"Thank you, ma'am."

More giggling. I try not to laugh. Looking at Damien isn't helping as I can him fight the same fight. He makes a face at me and that's all it takes. I burst out laughing, which does him in. After a few minutes, I regain my composure enough to speak.

"Sorry, but someone made a face at me," I say, pointing at Damien.

"I did no such thing,"

"Liar, liar, pants on fire."

"If my pants are on fire, it's because of you, babe."

I see Melissa roll her eyes while Judd smiles.

Looking over at Melissa, Judd says, "Gotta love these two."

"No way not to," Melissa replies.

The four of us sit there shooting the shit for a while longer until Judd gets up from the table.

"I had a great time, but I need to be gettin' to bed. Work starts early."

I swear I see drool come out of Melissa's mouth when he mentions bed.

"I should get going too," Melissa says as she stands up.

"May I walk you to your car, ma'am?" Judd asks.

He puts his arm out, which Melissa accepts.

"Thank you," she replies.

Damien and I stand together as we watch them walk out arm in arm. Damn, they look good together. We hear Melissa's car pull away and a few minutes later, Judd waves, then heads inside his house. Damien and I clean up, call the dogs over and head inside ourselves.

"Babe, are you sure you're okay after what I told you?"

"I am. If that's how she wants to be, that's her problem."

"That's my sexy woman."

"Mmmm," I say, wrapping my arms around him. I inhale, never tiring of the way his shower gel smells. He pulls me into a tight embrace and kisses me hard, his tongue running along my lips before exploring my mouth. I feel his erection growing against my leg, and I feel my favorite warming sensation spread between my thighs.

"I want you so fuckin' bad," Damien says.

"Take me to bed, now."

We get naked and get into bed. Damien's hands are all over me, exploring every inch of my flesh, setting my entire body on fire. Those hands are pure magic and I moan with every touch.

"Babe, I wanna see my sexy woman bouncing on my cock. Get that pretty pussy wrapped around me now!"

I decide to be a bit of a bad girl first and don't do as I'm told. Instead, I get on all fours and take his dick down my throat as he growls.

"Babe, that's not what I told you to do. What are we going to do about that?"

"You should spank me for that."

I feel his hand connect with my ass. The sweet sting makes me even wetter. I keep sucking his cock as he gives me a few more spanks, my pussy dripping with desire. I can't wait another second and I climb on top of him. I sit up, giving him a full view of my body wrapped around his cock as I fuck him hard. His hands make their way to my ass, massaging it.

"Fuck, babe, you look so damn hot. And shit, I can't get enough of your sexy ass. Fuck, it feels so good inside you. Babe, you fuck like no woman I've ever been with."

He takes one of his hands off my ass and starts massaging my clit, adding to my pleasure and pushing me to the edge. Wanting this to last, I change my pace, fucking him slower.

"You naughty little tease, you're driving me crazy, woman."

"Then tell me what you want me to do."

"Fuck me harder than ever before."

Damien puts his hands on my hips, helping me bounce harder. I lean back to get maximum stimulation on my g-spot and I feel my orgasm building faster than a freight train. My entire body convulses as I explode around him, drenching his dick,

"Oh, fuck, babe," he growls as he comes inside me, his body bucking beneath me.

I collapse down onto his chiseled chest, both of us drenched in sweat. Damien wraps his arms around me and kisses me. Being this close to him physically is incredible, not nothing compared to the feeling of being emotionally close to him.

"I need to say something."

"What's up, babe?"

"I'm sorry about earlier."

"Sorry for what?"

"I wigged when you talked about giving me the key. It's only because you caught me off guard. I've had some time to digest it, and if the offer still stands, I want the key."

"That makes me happy, but I want to make sure you know what I said earlier was a cover."

"I do, and thank you for that. I want this, and I want you. I love you, Damien."

"I love you, Lexi."

I let out an enormous yawn, spent after the hot fuck we just shared.

"Babe, how about we save party planning to tomorrow night?"

"Okay."

Chapter Twenty-Two

Damien

Saturday. Time to party and celebrate my sexy woman tonight. We're even going to have the amazing rock band Stardust in attendance. Wait until Lexi sees the surprise they helped me plan. Right now, she's out with Melissa, shopping for a new outfit for tonight. They're also going to get beautiful, as Melissa put it, whatever that means. My woman is already beautiful. I walk outside with Dave and see Judd.

"Howdy," Judd said. "Lookin' forward to tonight."

"Me too."

"Where's your pretty lady?"

"Out with Melissa getting ready."

I see a smile appear on Judd's face when I mention Melissa. Lexi believes they belong together. I've never understood women's obsessions with each other's love lives. I only give a fuck about who's in my bed. It will only ever be Lexi for me. I wipe the sweat off my brow. Summer is coming and I can't wait to spend it with my girl. Dave comes over to me and sits down, panting.

"I'll see ya later."

"Later, Judd."

After he finished his work, Judd stopped by and helped me get the backyard set up for tonight. We've transformed my backyard into a mini-rock concert venue. I have a rented stage and dance floor, along with plenty of tables and chairs. The kegs arrived, and I restocked the bar. Now, all that's left is for the caterer to get here and set up the food. I grab a quick shower and finish getting dressed just as the catering truck pulls into my driveway. I show them where to set up, then go back inside to wait for the ladies. About half an hour later, I hear a knock. I see Melissa standing there when I open the door, but no sign of Lexi.

"Please go take a seat on the couch and close your eyes," Melissa says.

I do as I'm told.

"When can I open them?"

"When I tell you."

"Okay."

I hear footsteps. Perfume fills the surrounding air.

"You can open your eyes now," I hear Melissa say.

My eyes pop open and I say nothing. My mouth forgets how to work. Instead, I just sit and stare.

"Told you," Melissa says to Lexi.

Lexi's hand waves in front of my face.

"Earth to Damien. Come in, Damien."

"Babe!"

Not giving a shit that Melissa's watching, I walk over to Lexi and grab her ass. Pulling her tight against me, I kiss her hard. She fills out that pair of jeans like they were made just for her. And holy fuck, the low-cut white t-shirt she's wearing could melt an iceberg. She's so fucking hot, I can barely control myself.

"While you ladies were out making yourselves even more drop-dead gorgeous, Judd and I were hard at work. Wait until you see the backyard."

The three of us walk outside. I look over at Lexi and see her eyes go wide.

"Wow, this is amazing."

"I agree. You guys did awesome," Melissa says.

I walk around the yard to make sure everything is set, while Lexi and Melissa hang back. A few minutes later, Melissa grabs onto Lexi for support, her mouth hanging open. I follow her gaze and see why.

"Hey, ya'll," Judd says.

His eyes go wide when he sees the ladies. We walk over to join them. He tips his hat to Melissa and her face turns red. Lexi frees herself from Melissa's grip and stands with me. Judd puts his arm out.

"May I escort you to a table?"

Melissa accepts his arm and giggles, but like the last time, no words come out. Judd and Melissa walk over to the table and sit down. Lexi looks at me and smiles.

"Call it a hunch, but I think Melissa is smitten," Lexi says.

"I don't think she's the only one. I saw the way Judd looked at her."

The rest of the guests arrive, including the members of Stardust and their wives. The band's road crew sets up their equipment on the stage while everyone drinks and mingles. The caterer lets me know that the food is all ready, so I walk to the stage and grab the mic.

"Thanks everyone for coming tonight. The food is ready, so please help yourselves."

After everyone else has been through the buffet line, Lexi and I grab our food. We join Melissa and Judd at their table. Once we finish eating, I turn some music on. I grab Lexi and take her to the dance floor. I love watching that sexy woman grind her hips. My dick stirs, and I have to talk him down. He'll have his fun later when I take that woman to bed.

Dusk rolls in, so I turn on the party lights that Judd helped me string up. Melissa pulls Lexi away for a minute, so I walk over to Mikael and Hannah.

"Are you ready to perform?" I ask Mikael.

"We are. Do you want us to pull Lexi up or do a couple of our songs first?"

"What do you think is better?"

"We'll warm the crowd up first, then play her song and call her up to sing with Dean."

"Sounds perfect. Thanks for doing this."

"If she's as talented as you said, she deserves to be heard."

"You won't be disappointed. I'll go introduce you now."

"Great. I'll let the boys know."

I walk up to the stage, grabbing Lexi on the way. I want her front and center for her surprise.

"Everyone, we have a special treat for you tonight. Please welcome the amazing Stardust to the stage."

The band walks on stage and gets into position. Dean grabs the microphone, counts off and the band plays. They played three songs to the roar of the party-goers.

"Thank you. For our next song, we're going to change things up and play a cover. We're going to need some help with this one. Lexi, join us on stage," Dean says.

Lexi looks at me and her eyes go wide. She shakes her head no. I will not allow her to chicken out.

"Babe, get that cute ass up on that stage."

I turn her around toward the stage. Dean is holding out his hand. Lexi takes his hand and walks up on stage. He cues the band, and I hear the opening notes of Me and Bobby McGee. Dean hands the microphone to Lexi and grabs his guitar. I watch my sexy woman take center stage. When her mouth opens, the crowd goes quiet. Everyone's mouth is hanging open, even Melissa, who's heard her before. When the song ended, the crowd erupted into the loudest applause I've ever heard.

Lexi bows, runs off stage, and straight into my arms. She has the biggest smile on her face, and my heart skips a beat.

"Thank you for that."

"What do you mean?"

"I know you set that up. You can deny it, but I know."

"Guilty."

"Guess I'll have to punish you later."

"Babe!"

Melissa and Judd walk over to join us. Melissa gives Lexi a hug.

"You were amazing," Melissa says.

"Thanks, girl."

"I agree. That's some set of pipes you have," Judd says.

"Thank you."

Stardust plays a couple more songs. When they finish up, I put the music back on and we all dance the night away. Lexi stays in my arms for the rest of the night. I can't wait to get her into bed later. After a couple more hours, the party winds down. Judd and Melissa are the last ones to leave. I smile as Judd escorts her to his car before he goes home. After I turn out the lights, Lexi and I race to my bedroom.

Chapter Twenty-Three

Lexi

"Get that hot ass over and kiss me, my naughty man."

He walks over and plants a kiss on me that makes my knees buckle. Fuck, I ache for his cock.

"Good. Now get naked and get in bed."

"Damn, babe."

"Less talkin', more strippin'!"

I stand there and let my eyes appreciate his breathtaking body. He lies down on the bed, dick at full attention. Slowly, I remove my clothes. He licks his lips as more of my flesh appears.

"Fuck, so sexy, babe."

I run my hands down my body as he watches. He grabs his dick and strokes himself. I flash him a smile as I walk to the bed and lie down next to him. Watching him stroking his cock is getting me hotter than hell. When I can't wait one more second, I grab his hand off his dick. After I mount him, I take his dick as deep inside my pussy as I can.

I slide up and down his cock with slow strokes. I savor every moment, as his dick touches the deepest parts of my body.

"Aren't you supposed to be punishing me?"

"I am. What do you want more than anything?"

"To feel you pound me hard and fast."

I look into his eyes and slow my pace even more. He narrows his eyes and tightens his mouth as he watches me. He tries to increase the pace, but I won't let him.

"No, no, no, Damien. We go at my pace tonight."

"Fuck, woman."

I sit up straight and rock my body on top of him. He watches me with his tongue hanging out as I fuck him slower than ever. I moan as every part of my pussy rubs against his erection. My body quakes. I'm desperate to increase my pace, but I'm determined to punish him for earlier. The pressure builds until I can't take another second. My body convulses as I explode around him. I forget where I am for a minute. This is the most intense pleasure I've felt yet, and I can't stop my body from quaking. Damien doesn't take his eyes off me.

"Please, babe, please fuck me."

I ride him faster this time, hearing him growl. I lose all control as I bounce hard. His body bucks beneath me as he comes inside me. I slide off him and lie down next to him. My body still tingles from my incredible orgasm.

"Babe, you were a natural up on stage tonight."

"I was a wreck."

"Well, you couldn't tell. You need to perform more."

"I would consider singing at the club. Will you join me?"

"Babe, I'll always be with you. I love you."

"I love you so much."

"Not sure about you, babe, but I'm exhausted."

"I am too, after that incredible fuck."

Damien nestles me in his arms and we fall asleep. The next morning, after we finished breakfast, we took the dogs out back to run. Damien's cell phones rings. I can only hear Damien's end of the conversation, and I try to figure out the rest.

"Hello."

"Thank you."

"We had fun too."

"Wow. Okay, I'll tell her."

"Later."

I look at Damien, but I don't ask him about the call. I'm not that girl.

"That was Mikael. He called to tell me how impressed he was with you. Dean called him this morning and told him they want to help you record a demo."

"Are you serious?"

"Babe, you're an incredible singer and everyone knows it. Everyone except for you. You need to do this."

"But"

"Stop. Not another word. If I have to put you over my shoulder and carry you into that studio, you will record that demo."

"I've only sung one song."

"Remember, Dean sings too. He knows what songs will suit your voice. Mikael said they will be at the studio this afternoon. We're welcome to stop by."

"Today? But that doesn't give me time to prepare."

"Let's go at least check it out."

"I don't know."

Damien pouts. I want to bite that lip. But it works.

"Okay."

He smiles. My knees buckle and I wrap my arms around him. I look at his face and lean in for a kiss. He twists his tongue around mine.

"I wanna go play with Mr. Big."

"Later, babe. We need to get ready to go."

"Fine."

Once we're dressed, we drive over to Dean's studio. I see Dean, Mikael, and their wives standing outside. Damien takes my hand and we walk over to join them.

"Welcome. We're glad you came. Follow us," Dean says.

Damien and I follow Dean and Mikael to a large building. My eyes go wide when Dean opens the door. This is the first time I've seen a studio, other than in pictures and videos. Dean takes us on a tour. He finishes in the recording booth. Mikael and Damien wait outside while I follow Dean in.

"I would like to try recording today."

"I guess."

"Don't be nervous. You have a special gift. Use it."

"I want to sing a different song."

"Great. I have something in mind."

"What? I want to make sure I know the words."

"Bad Reputation."

"I love that song. I know the lyrics by heart."

"Perfect. Put the headphones on to hear the track. Just sing at a normal volume. The microphone will take care of the rest. Remember, you don't have to sing perfectly on the first try. Take a deep breath."

"I'm ready."

Dean walks to the other room. I have a moment of panic, so I take a couple more deep breaths. I put the headphones on and hear the music start. When the song finishes, I look at Dean. He stands in the studio with a smile on his face. He motions me to join him. Damien and Mikael follow.

"Wow. You sounded incredible. Listen," Dean says.

He presses a button and I hear the song play. My jaw drops when I hear the vocal start. She has talent. Wait, that she is me. My voice sounds different in my head. I shake my head. That can't be me. Tears stream down my face and I look over at Damien.

"Babe, you fucking killed that."

"I agree," Mikael said.

"I thought we'd need a couple of takes, but Lexi, this is perfection," Dean said.

"Thank you."

"With your permission, I want our manager to hear this," Dean said.

"I don't know."

"Babe, it's incredible."

"Well, I guess. But if he hates it"

"Stop. I'm never letting you down yourself again, babe."

Images fill my head and tears sting my eyes. I can't do this. They're setting me up just like before. All I want to do is run away. I run to the door and out of the studio and I don't look back. I see a pond and I run until I reach out. I sink down onto the ground and bury my head in my hands. I thought I was over what happened that day.

Chapter Twenty-Four

Damien

I stand there trying to process what just happened. I look at Dean and Mikael, unsure of what to say.

"What just happened?" Dean asked.

"No idea," I said.

"Go after her, man," Mikael said.

"Let me talk to her."

We turn around and see Hannah.

"Alex and I saw her run out of the studio."

We watch Hannah and Alex sit on either side of Lexi. They each wrap an arm around her. The three of them talk for quite a while until I see them all get up and head back to the studio. All three of them have smiles on their faces as they enter the studio.

"I'm so sorry," Lexi says.

I see Hannah nod to Mikael and Dean. The three of them and Alex all walk out.

"Babe, talk to me."

"I'm sorry. They must think I'm an ass,"

"Not at all. Tell me what happened."

Lexi sits on the couch, and I join her.

"When I was a freshman, a couple of girls talked me into trying out for the cheerleading team. I said no, but she insisted I was perfect for the team. I wasn't. Dancing and gymnastics are not two of my talents. The other girls laughed at me and insulted me. The whole thing was a setup. I didn't think so then, but I now believe Amy was behind it."

I wrap my arms around Lexi and hug her tight. She lays her head on my shoulder and I feel drops on my arm.

"They told me I wouldn't fit into a uniform; that I was too fat to do gymnastics. They also said that if I danced, it would feel like an earthquake. Amy covered up her part in the scheme. I was so desperate for friends that I let her. I thought I was over it, but after what happened recently with Amy, it's come back."

"And Melissa never said a word?"

"She didn't know. She was out because of a death in the family. I never told her, never told anyone. At least not until today. Talking with Alex and Hannah helped."

"Thank you for trusting me enough to tell me."

"Thank you for helping me find courage. I want Dean to give the recording to his manager."

I jump up and pull Lexi up.

"Let's tell them."

Lexi and I walk outside. I see the other couples at the pond, so we join them.

"Dean, I've decided I want your manager to listen."

"Awesome. I'll call him tomorrow."

"Thanks."

"Thanks for everything, man," I say to Dean.

"You got it. Now, get that diva home."

Lexi blushes as we all laugh. I take her hand and we walk to my car.

"Babe, I'm so proud of you. Now, how about Chinese food and Netflix for the rest of the night?"

"Sounds perfect."

Once we get home, we make plates of food and park our asses in front of the TV. We decide to unwind with some episodes of The Office. I put my arm around Lexi and she lays her head on my shoulder.

"Babe, I can't stop thinking what you told me earlier. I'm angry that anyone did that to you."

"It was my fault. I knew I wasn't cheerleader material, but I tried out anyway."

"No, it wasn't your fault. Those bitches did this to you. And we're going to get them back."

"What do you mean?"

"We're going to show them how amazing you are. I'm taking you to your reunion and you're going to sing."

"I can't do that."

"Like hell. And you will have Stardust backing you up."

"I don't understand."

"I'm going to talk to them about playing the reunion and calling you up on stage to sing with them. Not only will the sexiest rockstar ever escort you be escorted to the reunion, you also get to sing with an amazing band. We'll show those bitches."

"I don't know what I would do without you."

"You'll never have to find out. You're stuck with me, babe."

"Good. I can't think of a single person on this planet that I would rather be with."

Her words affect me in ways I never could have imagined. I stand up and pull her up into my arms. Without a word, I scoop her up and carry her to bed. We've fucked countless times since we met, but tonight, something's different. She was so open with me earlier, and it made me love her even more. Tonight, all I want is to make love to her. I put her down and walk over to the bed.

"Come to me, babe."

She joins me and I pull her close. I kiss her beautiful lips and I feel her open for me. Our tongues intertwine as we kiss. I break the kiss long enough to lift her shirt off and toss it aside. I feel her hands under my shirt, and she lifts it off. I love her soft skin against mine. I slide her bottoms and panties down, and she steps out of them. Fuck, she looks so damn hot. I remove my shorts and again, scoop her up. I lay her down on the bed and lay down next to her.

Leaning over her, I kiss her. She wraps her arms around me, her hands landing on my back. My mouth finds her neck, and I savor the taste of her skin. I slide my fingers between her breasts, followed by my tongue. I straddle her and run my tongue down her belly. She moans as my tongue finds her sweet pussy. I focus on her clit until her body quakes.

"Oh, Damien, it feels so good. I'm coming. Please don't stop."

Her body bucks beneath me as she finishes her orgasm, and I hear her sigh. I slide up her body and slide my dick inside her pussy, still slick from her orgasm. I hold her tight, kissing her beautiful mouth as we make love. Nothing feels as incredible as her warm pussy wrapped around my cock. My pulse quickens as I near climax and I thrust harder. I love how her skin feels, so soft and warm. I empty myself inside her.

"I love you, Alexis."

"I love you, Damien."

I roll off of her and pull her into my arms. She lays her head on my chest, and I stroke her hair. Even drenched in sweat, hair matted to her forehead, she's still the most beautiful woman I've even seen. I don't want another morning to arrive without me waking up next to her.

"Move in with me."

Her eyes go wide.

"What?"

"Babe, I love waking up with you next to me. I want that every single day. Please, move in with me."

"But, Maggie."

"I have plenty of room. Maggie and Dave get along great."

"I love it here."

"Then there's only one answer."

She says nothing, and my heart sinks. Did I ask too soon? Did I put too much pressure on her? I'm such an asshole. I'm so busy berating myself that I almost miss her answer.

"Yes."

"What did you just say, babe?"

"Yes. I'll move in with you."

I jump up on the bed. I look down at Lexi and her mouth is hanging open. I hold my hands out to her.

"What?" she asks.

"Get your ass up here."

She gets up and stands in front of me. I hold out my hands again, and she takes them. I jump up and down on the bed.

"What the hell are you doing?" she asks.

"Celebrating. Now join me."

Holding hands, we jump up and down on the bed like two kids. We're still naked, so her naked breasts are bouncing like crazy. She loses her balance and ends up on her ass on the bed. I pretend to do the same, and both of us erupt in laughter. She pushes me onto my back and straddles me. I feel her grab my dick and slide it inside of her. We fuck hard and fast until we come together. We're both so spent, we drift off to sleep.

We spend the next several weeks packing up Lexi's stuff and moving it in into my house. We're sitting on the couch watching TV when my phone rings. I see Dean's number on my screen.

"Hello."

"Hey man, sorry for the delay, but my manager finally listened to Lexi's song."

"Putting you on speaker."

"Hey Lexi, Xander listened to your recording and asked me to share his feedback."

I hear Lexi sigh.

"Okay, let me have it."

To be continued...

Afterword

What feedback does Xander have for Lexi? What else is in store for our lovers? Find out in Rockin' Summer, due out June 20, 2022.

About the Author

Samantha Michaels was born in 1973 in the small town of Abington, PA and was raised and still lives in Hatboro, PA (both suburbs of Philadelphia). She is married to her high school sweetheart and they have a rescue dog, a beautiful Black Lab named Holly.

When she's not writing or working at her full-time job, she enjoys watching her Philly sports team (hopefully) win, listening to heavy metal/hard rock music, reading, and spending time with friends and family.

Her love of reading began at a young age, thanks to her mother and Sesame Street. Her mom read to her constantly, and by three years old, she was reading on her own, and hasn't stopped. This eventually turned into a love of writing. She was writing for herself and then for a small group of friends, one of whom told her she should be writing books. She took her friends advice and has since published several romance books with plenty more on the way.

Also by Samantha Michaels

The Rockstar Quadrilogy

Leather and Lace

A Second Shot at Love

Pet Shop Passion

Silent Angel - Coming April 2022

The Melody of the Seasons

Rockin' Spring

Rockin' Summer - Coming June 2022

Rockin' Autumn - Coming September 2022

Rockin' Winter - Coming December 2022

www.ingramcontent.com/pod-product-compliance
Lightning Source LLC
Chambersburg PA
CBHW020152180626
46810CB00004B/1859